"You're here," I said, reaching in for the group hug I didn't realize I needed until it was right in front of me.

"And we always will be," said Reagan.

"Now let's get you home. I'll let you decide if you want a margarita tonight or tomorrow on the way to your place."

"How about sleep tonight and margarita tomorrow?"

"Perfect. Sounds like the best excuse for Nacho Night In at my place. And Rebecca will be able to join too," said Reagan.

Good, I thought. Maybe by then I'd find the courage to tell them all that the head of our global RFP and data team was leaving soon, and I was thinking about campaigning for a promotion to her job and moving to London permanently. As for tonight, I really just needed to curl into my bed and let Mariah sing me to sleep.

Dear Reader,

Have you ever felt that every piece of your life is going right except the one thing you want the most? If so, I think you'll relate to Robin Johnson, a massively successful, dynamic woman who never settles for anything less than the best—including in love. This has served her well in her career, her fashion choices and even with her new apartment, which seems like it was built out of a fantasy world and made just for her. But when it comes to love, Robin's no-convincing motto has unfortunately resulted in a lot of dates, plenty of lonely nights, even more heartbreak and a fear that maybe she's just not meant to find romantic love.

Thankfully, she has her best friends by her side— Reagan, Jennifer, Rebecca and her UK guidepost, Oliva—as she journeys to London for a new promotion. With them in her corner, Robin learns to navigate friendships on both sides of the Atlantic Ocean and finds a partner who helps her feel seen, sexy and safe being vulnerable.

London Calling is the third novel in The Friendship Chronicles series. It's a heartwarming, sometimes steamy, look at what it takes to believe in love again. Featuring many of your favorites from *The Shoe Diaries* and *Bloom Where You're Planted*, this book follows Robin as she looks to start a new life with hopes of a new shot at love in the newest place she's calling home.

Hope you enjoy!

Darby Baham

London Calling

DARBY BAHAM

HARLEQUIN
SPECIAL
EDITION

Recycling programs
for this product may
not exist in your area.

ISBN-13: 978-1-335-72421-2

London Calling

Copyright © 2022 by Darby Baham

For questions and comments about the quality of this book, please contact us at CustomerService@Harlequin.com.

Harlequin Enterprises ULC
22 Adelaide St. West, 41st Floor
Toronto, Ontario M5H 4E3, Canada
www.Harlequin.com

Printed in U.S.A.

Darby Baham (she/her) is a proud New Yorker of six years who has had personal blog posts appear in the *Washington Post*'s relationship vertical, plus *Blavity*, *FEMI Magazine* and more. She's also worked in the communications industry for more than two decades. Originally from New Orleans, LA, Darby lived in the Washington, DC, area for fifteen years, where she cultivated a beautiful, sprawling shoe closet and met some of the best people in her orbit. Her debut novel, *The Shoe Diaries*, was released January 2022. The follow-up, *Bloom Where You're Planted*, was released May 2022.

Books by Darby Baham

Harlequin Special Edition

The Friendship Chronicles

The Shoe Diaries
Bloom Where You're Planted

Visit the Author Profile page
at Harlequin.com for more titles.

To all the people in my life who still give me hope
for the most passionate, endearing, honest,
specific love made just for me—thank you.
Your love stories and experiences are what inspire me
to write the words that I pray remind others to
never stop believing they deserve all that and more.

Part 1

"Give a girl the right shoes, and she can conquer the world."

—Marilyn Monroe

Prologue

"It's just not working, Eric."

I held back my tears, hating that breaking up was how I was spending my last night in London. It certainly wasn't what I'd planned when I touched down just two weeks before.

"But it can," he responded, his piercing blue eyes looking at me as if he wanted to get up, come over to me and beg me to change my mind. Instead, he remained seated, dignified, of course, and stared daggers in my direction from across the living room. "If we really want it to, it can."

Perched on a stool by my kitchenette island, I desperately wanted to get up as well, reassure him and take back what I'd said, but I knew in my heart I couldn't.

"No, I don't think so," I said.

My words came out barely louder than a whisper, but I was resolute. It took every fiber of courage I had in me to stick with them, though, especially as I watched Eric hunch over slightly on the chaise lounge that came with my flat. I could see that he genuinely wanted us to be together, but as glamorous as dating a member of the royal family had been, I didn't want it anymore. What I wanted, instead, was something that maybe seemed simple in comparison but what I'd come to realize Eric could never give me—a real relationship that allowed me to be fully myself and fully loved, flaws and all.

And while this recent trip had been intended to be just like all my other work trips to London—I'd spend a few weeks working late hours and traipsing through the city after all—it had also given me the aha moments I'd needed about Eric and the city itself. For one, I could now finally admit that no matter how many times or ways I tried it, I didn't like blood sausage. Blame it on my American taste buds or something, but the truth was, when it came to English food, I'd rather someone point me in the direction of the nearest Jamaican spot than the closest pub with fish and chips.

Also, I was finally confident in naming some of my favorite UK things—like waking up on a Saturday afternoon, rolling out of bed, getting dressed and making my way to afternoon tea at Harrods. I'm talking smoked salmon sandwiches, praline spheres, lemon meringue tarts, baked scones and the finest tea offerings one can imagine. Or even, despite it being a huge tourist trap, taking a whirl on the London Eye whenever I had the chance, especially when a friend visited, so I could use them as an excuse to see the city from up high.

I'd learned two more things on this trip: (1) that I was growing tired of coming to London for a couple weeks at a time every few months, but not in the way I might have expected. Instead of clamoring to get back to DC full-time, I was starting to consider what it might be like to make London my home. And yet (2), I couldn't picture Eric in my life once I returned. Sadly, as lovely as he was, and even though we'd been together for several months, Eric had never even been able to even join me for any of the things that made me love London. Instead, all we ever did was talk about all the things we wanted to do together and then occasionally have secret rendezvouses in the countryside and dates in my apartment—all of which were great and romantic, but not real.

The last realization meant I had to make the devastating decision to end things, which was no easy feat, considering I was thirty years old and still no closer to finding lasting love. Plus, who breaks up with a literal prince? I just knew my friends back home were going to be so disappointed; after seeing him ride up to us in a horse-led carriage in May, they'd already started calling us the new Harry and Meghan—just with, hopefully, slightly less racism, since Eric was far removed from anyone's line of succession.

"So, it's really just over?" Eric asked, breaking the awkward silence between us and my rambling thoughts. "It's that easy for you? I risked a lot to date you—you know that."

"I know," I quickly responded, slightly offended that that's what he felt was important to bring up in this conversation, but also realizing he was a man speaking in pain. "And, of course, it's not easy."

I leaned my body toward him, as if that would somehow show him that he wasn't the only one in the room hurting.

"Do you know that before our first date, I tried on at least twenty outfits before settling on something because I was so excited to go out with you?" I asked him, holding back my tears. "The way you looked at me when you first introduced yourself inspired all the girly giggles that I didn't know I had inside me. You gave me hope again, Eric. I wanted so desperately for this—" I paused and swung my arms out wide, gesturing at him and the secret life we'd built in my temporary flat. "All of this...to be real. But as much as we wanted things to be different, this relationship has always been predicated on a fantasy. You know that. It's built on this idea that I would come to London every few months, upending my actual life, and then we'd get to spend this magical time in the flat that's not truly mine all because we can't go out in the real world out of precaution that you'll be seen with someone, and the British press will pounce on the story. I want more than that. I—I know you do, too."

It felt almost as if I was in a play reciting a monologue—I just kept droning on and on. But I had to somehow get it across to Eric that I wasn't making this decision lightly. And while I was the friend always at the ready to protect others, I'd had real hopes that he was finally going to be the person I could count on to protect *me*. It brought me no solace realizing he wasn't.

"I want you," he said with a sigh.

"And I *wanted* you. But not like this."

"I can't change who I am, Robin. You knew who I was when you started dating me."

"And I don't want to change you, Eric. I promise. I just know this isn't for me. I'm sorry."

I brought my hands to my temples, trying to rub away the tension I felt building inside me.

"So, what now?" he asked, still seated as far away from me as possible.

"Now," I said, bringing my hands back to down to my legs, "I guess I go back to my life in DC, and you go back to yours in the palace."

I shrugged, not out of defeat, but more out of uncertainty at any other outcome for us.

"And if you come back to London, *when* you come back to London, am I just supposed to pretend you don't exist?"

"It's what normal people do all the time when they break up," I said, half chuckling. "We watch the other person's social media for a while, we have moments where we wish we could tell them something we know they'd want to hear and then we slowly but surely start to move on. I think that's the best course of action for us."

"You're probably right. That certainly does not mean I have to like it."

"If it's any consolation, it'll be loads harder for me to forget you existed, you know, with you being a prince and all. I can't just avoid your social media. I have to avoid the news!"

"If there's one thing I'm certain of, Robin Bridget Johnson, it's that it will take me a lot longer to forget you than the other way around."

Eric paused, looking as if he was trying to figure out what he should say next.

"I do wish you the best, however," he finally blurted out. "And I hope you find the relationship that you want."

"Thank you, Eric. I hope you do, too. Genuinely."

With another sigh, he stood and walked toward me, wrapping me tightly in his broad arms. I could feel the way his chest moved up and down through his button-down shirt and wanted to hold on as long as I could—remembering all the times we'd laughed together and knowing I'd never be this close to his heartbeat again.

"I'm going to miss you so much," I admitted, my head buried in his chest. "I really wish—"

"It's okay," he said and then silently kissed my forehead before breaking our embrace. Mouthing *goodbye* as he walked to my door to leave, Eric gave me one final glance and then never looked back.

As soon as the door closed behind him, I fell to my knees and let all the tears I'd been holding in come crashing out. I couldn't help fearing that I'd just passed on my one last chance at love.

* * *

The following day, my flight landed at Dulles International Airport in Virginia at approximately 7:00 p.m. Eastern. My eyes were still red and my face was bloated, but I was home and ready to sleep off the hurt that suddenly seemed like it would never go away. Sure, I was the one who broke up with Eric, but that didn't make it any easier. I still missed him and the hope I felt of having found love with him. About the only thing that kept me from embarrassing myself with loud sobs the entire flight back was the Mariah Carey playlist that I had booming through my earbuds. Over the years, I'd used her music to keep me going whenever I needed to feel inspired before a big workday, get over a heartbreak or even have something in my ears that perfectly described the joy I felt.

Plus, she was an Aries like me, so obviously we had a connection. And after an incredibly hard breakup that I'd had to go through with for my peace of mind, her music was the only thing that I knew that could help me remain confident in my decision—I mean, what was "Vision of Love" about if not about a woman realizing that her dream of the relationship was not synonymous with reality and then believing that she would eventually find a love that suited her best? I needed that reminder more than ever.

By the time I grabbed my blush-pink Michael Kors suitcase and matching weekender bag from baggage claim and exited customs, the sun had already started to set, which made perfect sense as far as I was concerned. I didn't need a sunny welcome back to the

States when I felt anything but happy and full of sunshine. The change in the sky was also somehow a great reminder that I needed to let my parents and my girls know that I'd landed safely. Securing my bags in one hand, I started by texting my parents, the oh-so-happily-married Johnsons who never seemed to argue unless they were discussing why their only child just couldn't seem to keep a man.

Hey Mom & Dad! Just letting you know I made it back to DC safely.

Mom: Oh, thank goodness! How was your flight back?

It wasn't too bad. I'm just ready to get in bed now.

Mom: I can imagine. I hope you get some good rest tonight, dear.

Dad: Welcome back, sweetie. Hey, tell your mom I'm right. Didn't Eric surprise you with a cabin full of camellias on your last trip? Your mom swears it was peonies, but I told her peonies are Jennifer's favorite flower... yours are camellias.

Aren't you two sitting next to each other right now, Dad?

Dad: Yeah...so?

So, why don't you tell her yourself?

Dad: I did! But she's not remembering right and doesn't believe me. I was telling her that boy is a keeper because he knows my baby girl so well and how she needs a romantic fella in her life.

I sighed and contemplated putting my phone on silent and back in my purse so I could avoid what I was sure was coming next. While my best friends, Reagan and Jennifer, and even my newest friend, Rebecca, knew I was planning to break up with Eric, I hadn't found the heart to tell my parents yet. Not when they were so excited about me "finally finding love," as they had not-so-casually mentioned more than once. There was no sense in dragging out my torture, however, so I bit down on my lip, loosened my grip on my luggage and ripped off the text Band-Aid.

Well, Dad, the thing is… I broke up with Eric last night.

Dad: What?!

Mom: Oh no no no no, sweetie.

Dad: Did he do something to hurt you?

Mom: Why would you just assume he did something wrong?

Dad: Well, who breaks up with a prince if it's not because he did something wrong?

Okay, this is my cue to leave, I texted back quickly, hoping to avoid any further discussion about my love life with my parents one day after my breakup. Besides, if I let them, they were surely going to try to engage in a debate about me in front of me—but over text. I didn't have the heart for it.

I love you both, but I need to call my Uber so I can get home and just sleep.

Mom: Okay, baby, you're right. We're sorry.

Dad: Yes, your mom and I just want...you know what? Never mind. Get home safely and call us in the morning.

Mom: And we love you, too.

Dad: Yes, we do.

I was willing to bet good money they were probably continuing their decade-plus argument in the comforts of my childhood living room, but they'd have to do it without me tonight. Completely drained from my travels and my breakup, I didn't have the energy to once again remind them that they'd done a wonderful job raising up an incredibly confident woman who was succeeding as a marketing manager in the wild world of global investment management and who didn't need a partner to prove her worth. I also wasn't quite sure I'd fully believe my go-to speech for them at the moment, anyway.

After taking a deep breath to compose myself, I grabbed my bags again and started making my way toward the ride app pickup section. I'd long ago realized it was best to wait until I was closer to that section to request my ride, because the last thing anyone wanted after a long flight from London was having to run to catch their car before the four-minute grace period ended. But two steps away from my usual marker in the airport, when I'd feel comfortable enough to make my Uber request, I heard someone shout out my nickname. There were only three people in the world who called me Rob, so I instantly knew who it had to be before I ever saw them. And yet, when I looked up and caught Jennifer and Reagan waving a sign at me like the chauffeurs who pick up the celebrities at the airport, I smiled for the first time in at least twenty-four hours.

"I can't believe you all are here. What are you doing here?" I asked, trying to contain my excitement.

"We knew you'd need us," said Jennifer.

"So, we're here," added Reagan, expertly chiming in to finish her sentence, just like the three of us had been doing since we met at Howard University. Back then our original quartet included our friend Christine, who was quite possibly the best human being I'd ever known. And we'd been inseparable—with Reagan and Christine coming from New Orleans, me being from Chicago, and Jennifer, my bestie from California, rounding out the group. In truth, we weren't that much alike, but somehow, we complemented each other perfectly. Rae was the charming five-foot-three stiletto lover and perfectionist, Jenn was the sweetheart who wore everyone else's heart on her sleeve, and Chrissy was the raspy-voiced Afro-Latina opera singer who managed to be the life of every party she entered— even the jazz processional after her funeral last year.

These days, Rebecca, whom we called Becs, rounded out our foursome, coming into the fold after befriending Reagan at work. What had started off as a nice enough work friendship had fully blossomed into a connection that none of us were able to deny. She was part of us now, and in truth, we'd needed her passion for life that much more as Chrissy began to slip away and eventually pass from complications due to her chronic illness.

"You're here," I said, reaching in for the group hug I hadn't realized I needed until it was right in front of me.

"And we always will be," said Jennifer. "Now, let's get you home. I'll let you decide when we're on the way to your place if you want a margarita tonight or tomorrow."

I didn't need that long to know my answer.

"How about sleep tonight and margarita tomorrow?" I responded, hoping they would be understanding.

"Of course. We'll do whatever works for you," added Reagan. "And anyway, that's perfect. Sounds like the best excuse for Nacho Night at my place. Rebecca will be able to join then, too."

"Yes, to Nacho Thursdays—" started Jenn.

"On a Saturday!" I said in unison with Reagan.

"Just as it should be," Jennifer said, laughing.

"One day we will actually do them on a Thursday again," remarked Reagan.

"Yeah, but it's so much more fun when we don't," Jennifer replied, still giggling and bringing us to laughter because she simply couldn't stop.

Good, I thought to myself. There was nothing more comforting than a Saturday night version of Nacho Thursdays with my girls to help me get back to who I was—the woman who loved strongly, worked her ass off and never, ever took any crap from anyone. Maybe by the time we were all full of margaritas and tortilla chips doused in cheese and meat I might also find the courage to tell everyone that the head of our global RFP, marketing and data team was leaving soon, and I was thinking about campaigning for a promotion to her job—which would mean moving to London permanently.

But for tonight, I really just wanted to curl into my bed and let Mariah sing me to sleep.

Chapter One

Seven months later, I was back at Dulles International Airport. Same Michael Kors suitcases and blond balayage lob in tow, but this time I was on my way to London with no return flight. In celebration of my big move, I was also rocking the Sophia Webster Evangeline angel wing sandals that Reagan gave me during our joint thirtieth birthday party. The black suede–and–rose gold heels featured a four-inch metallic stiletto, but the pièce de resistance was the rose gold wings that extended from the back of the shoe, where the ankle strap wrapped delicately around my leg. I'd paired them with a pair of acid-washed skinny jeans that stopped just above my ankles and a T-shirt that read Black, Chic and Educated topped with a blush-pink blazer and a white–and–navy blue polka dot trench coat that tied at my waist, flared out and stopped just below my knees.

In all honesty, it probably was not what most people would consider proper attire for a seven-plus-hour flight overseas, but if there was a good time to make the airport my runway, campaigning for and getting the promotion that was sending me to London full-time was the exact right occasion.

Besides, I had plenty of time to saunter leisurely to my gate, since I always arrived at airports with at least two hours to spare—at least in the last few years. Even with TSA PreCheck, I once found myself running for and not catching a flight back home, and I'd vowed to never make that mistake again. My friends, who always clowned me for being just late enough to make a grand entrance (anywhere between one to five minutes late, which they deemed "being on RBJ time"), never understood this side of me. But they weren't with me when I arrived at my gate in Dubai two minutes after they closed the doors. That's not an experience you forget or ever want to repeat.

This time around, after going through security, I made my way to &pizza, a fast-casual restaurant that began in DC and was known for its oblong-shaped customizable pizzas. While I knew I'd be flying back to the States at some point for various important events, like Jennifer's upcoming bridal shower, I also knew it would be a while before I had the opportunity for &pizza again. So, as I walked up to the counter to place my order, I already had in mind that this was cause for a splurge.

"Hi, how are you?" I asked the guy behind the counter with a Midwestern smile plastered on my face.

"I'm doing great. And you?"

His not-quite-Southern-but-sort-of-twangy accent immediately told me he was born and raised in DC, unlike me and so many others who called it home only after coming for college and staying.

"I'm doing pretty well," I responded and then caught the twinkle in his eyes as he followed my outfit from head to toe.

"Oh sis, you are doing very well. Hello?!"

"Please, don't make me blush," I said with a quiet giggle. "I don't normally go all out like this for the airport, but I'm moving to London, so…"

"Say less, sis," my new best friend said, interrupting me. "I am here for you and this whole thing you have going on."

He swung his hand around in a circle as he said, "this whole thing," serving to both punctuate the end of his sentence and express just how much of my outfit he meant. Then, with a snap, he leaned in a little closer and whispered, "Do you want to be my sugar mama?"

"Only if you can get me the sugar daddy first! I can't help you before I help me," I replied, my giggle turning into a full-on laugh, snort and all.

"You know what? You are too much! But I love you anyway…and yes, I mean that already."

I continued cracking up. This kind of rapport was something I was probably going to miss about DC. When I moved here from Chicago, I'd initially heard people say that the residents were mean, but I'd always found it to be quite the opposite—if you are dynamic with them, most people will return the favor. And lucky for me, I was blessed with enough confidence and snark to go around, mixed with the Southern feel of a lot of Black people from the Midwest, since our grandparents and great-grandparents grew up in Mississippi, Louisiana and Alabama.

"What can I get you, though?" he asked, ultimately bringing us back to the main reason I'd come to &pizza in the first place.

"Oh! Yes, okay—so I want a traditional pizza with classic tomato sauce, fresh and shredded mozzarella, spinach, shrimp, pepperoni, beef meatballs, bacon, olive oil, and olives."

He walked through the different stations behind the counter, adding each of the ingredients as I said them aloud, and finally looked up when there was literally no room left on my pizza.

"No judgment," I said quickly as I caught his eyes. "Remember, I'm leaving! I have to do it big since it will be a *loooong* time before I can have this again."

"No judgment from me, Miss Mamas," he said with a wink. "But those cute skinny jeans might be angry with you after."

"Don't worry, I plan on getting very comfortable once I'm on the plane—I'm talking secretly unbuckling the jeans and exchanging my heels for my fuzzy slippers, the whole nine. This entire outfit is for departing and arriving purposes only."

"Oh. Well, then eat on!" He slipped my pizza into

the oven and proceeded to check me out while we waited.

"Can I ask what the fancy new job is?" he asked as I dipped my credit card into the machine.

"Of course!" I exclaimed with a joking flip of my hair. "So, I've been working for the same global investment management group for about four years now, and I was most recently the marketing manager for the requests for proposal team in the US, but that team included people who worked on global and international accounts, too."

I could see his eyes starting to gloss over, so I tried my best to switch to layman's terms. It was something I was used to doing when trying to explain what I worked on to, well, anyone who wasn't also in investments. It was just a little difficult to explain the intricacies of my promotion without giving him some of the nitty-gritty, too, though. Still, I was determined to try.

"This means I've had the pleasure of traveling to London every few months or so to learn about new products," I said, clearing my throat and then continuing. "Well, the last time I was in London, my supervisor—who ran the global RFP, marketing and data team—informed me that she was resigning soon to spend more time with her family. She basically told me that if I wanted it, I was a shoo-in for her job. And I guess I wanted it," I said, concluding my explanation with a shrug, my smile steadily increasing as I heard the accomplishment flow out of my own lips.

"Okay, so all I heard was 'I was a big deal before

and made a lot of money and now I'm about to make even more money,' honey."

"Yes, well something like that," I said, finding myself continuing to giggle with this man whose name I only knew because he had a pin on his shirt proclaiming it.

"Don't get shy now," said Brian. "Those Sophia Webster heels already told me I was talking to big money. This just confirmed it."

"Wait. How did you know—?"

He interrupted me again before I could finish my question.

"Okay, I'm offended that you would think I wouldn't know," he said, with a sly grin.

"You know what? You're right. My bad. Let me take my pizza and go in the corner and eat it in shame."

"Never that," he said, as he boxed it into its own personal pizza container. "You are a badass. And I already told you I'm in love, so I wouldn't let you slink away even if you tried."

"Well, thank you. And just so you know, these shoes were a gift from one of my best friends. I did *not* buy them myself."

"No longer listening to your excuses, Miss Mamas. You go eat that pizza so that you can sashay your fancy butt to that plane on time and take London by storm."

"Thanks, B," I said, giving him a nickname and a wink for his encouragement—my signature way of disarming or validating the people around me.

As I walked to a table to sit down and eat, I took a moment to really enjoy the sound of being called a

badass, even if it was by a total—extremely kind—
stranger. It wasn't lost on me that those were the same
words Reagan had used in her note when she gifted
me the shoes that were now carrying me to my new
journey.

Okay, I could be a badass, I thought. *Let's do this.*

Nearly twelve hours later, I found myself in the back
seat of my cab leaving Heathrow airport and heading
to my flat, the gray sky barely letting the morning sun
peek out. Despite my job being in London's financial district, aka The City, I'd made what some might
consider an impractical decision and chosen a flat in
Westminster—closeish to the Elizabeth Tower, Big
Ben, Harrods and, of course, my favorite—the London
Eye. I knew it wasn't where most people chose to live;
in fact, any time I'd visited in the past, I stayed in one
of the company's flats a couple blocks away from my
office building. But this time around, I figured (1) I
could afford it, and (2) if I was going to move to London full-time, I wanted to be in the midst of so many
of the things I loved. Lucky me, I found a beautiful flat
in Vincent Square, within relative walking distance of
all the tourism hot spots. Unluckily for me, this also included Buckingham Palace, but I figured it was worth
the calculated risk—chances were slim I'd run into Eric
casually strolling along the street.

Still brimming with excitement despite the long
flight, I decided to make one pit stop before heading
to my new flat. Almost like it was calling my name
and drawing me to it, I could hear the bustling crowd

of Parliament Square in my head the moment I stepped onto English soil. I knew instantly that my first destination had to be there so that I could take a photo with my bags, my fancy heels, one of London's iconic red phone booths and Big Ben in the background. And oddly enough, the hour-long ride from Heathrow did nothing to squelch this excitement; all I had left to do was hope that the typically busy area would be relatively calm enough this morning for me to be able to set up the timer on my phone, take some photos and not worry about anyone stealing my stuff as I played photographer and model in one.

As we got closer to the square, I found myself staring out the cab window and watching with glee as we passed by attraction after popular attraction. You'd think it was my first time in London by the way I was reacting, but in many ways, it felt like it, because it was the very first time that I was coming back to it as my home. When we rounded the bend near the Wellington Arch and turned onto Constitution Hill—the bright green grass of Buckingham Palace Garden and Green Park flanking us on the right and left—I knew we were mere steps away from famous landmarks such as the palace and Princess Diana's memorial walk. And it almost felt like the universe was saying "welcome home" as we drove down the beautiful, tree-lined streets leading us right to the red phone booth waiting for my impromptu photo shoot.

About a block away, my driver pulled over to let me out.

"I'm sorry I can't you get any closer, but the traffic over there will be terribly difficult for me to stop my car," he said.

"No need to apologize. I completely understand," I replied, offering him one of my signature winks while paying for my ride. "Besides, walking around the city is part of being a Londoner, right?"

I lifted my weekender bag onto my shoulder and climbed out of the car. By the time I comfortably stood up in my heels and joined him near the trunk, he'd already grabbed my suitcase and was waiting for me.

"Thanks so much," I said.

"You're welcome, miss. I hope your photos come out really nice."

"I do, too," I exclaimed, holding back the excited yelp that wanted to come pouring out of my throat. I was finally here and ready to plant my flag like every millennial across the world does—with a beautifully curated Instagram post.

With one bag on my shoulder and my roller suitcase secured in my left hand, I watched as the driver got back into his car and drove off and then looked up toward Big Ben as my guiding star. It only took me a few minutes before I walked right up to the row of phone booths I had in mind. With either of these, I'd be able to take photos inspired by all the photographers and painters over the years who had showcased London with the singular image of a red phone booth perfectly positioned with Big Ben and the Elizabeth Tower on its left shoulder. Thankfully, I found an empty one and set up shop, my hair flowing in the cold January wind, but my determination to capture the perfect image guiding my every move.

Using the tall handle on my suitcase, I propped my phone up with the timer set for ten seconds and the camera set to take multiple photos with one click. And then, like a track star preparing for a race, I clicked the white circle in the camera app of my phone and walked as fast as I could in my heels back to the phone booth before the timer went off. I had two seconds to spare and then it was go time. There I was, striking pose after pose, doing my best to imitate the dynamic posing my photographer friends had all tried to teach me—pausing just enough to allow the camera to catch me but flowing steadily with my movements. In some poses, I laughed hysterically, in others I played with my blond-streaked hair as it lightly touched the edge of my shoulders and in others, I was the coolest traveler around with her weekender bag delicately swinging off her fingertips.

All told, I probably took about two hundred photos in a matter of ten minutes—but I only needed one for the 'Gram. And after scrolling through my phone for what felt like forever, I found it—the perfect pose to announce my London arrival. I quickly shared it to my Instagram app with a simple caption: Hello London, goodbye DC. #nofilter #yearof30 #faithoverfears.

That out of the way, I scooped up my bags once again and decided it was probably best to hail a new taxi to get to my flat. While I was all for becoming a true Londoner and learning to walk everywhere, I also knew that Vincent Square was about a twenty-minute walk from where I was, and if I did any more physical activity in these heels, Reagan was likely to disown me. As an only child, I couldn't afford to get disowned by any of my friends—jokingly or not.

Chapter Two

The entrance hallway of my flat was furnished with one of the largest cherry-oak–framed mirrors I'd ever seen. Situated right underneath it was a white entry table that featured a shelf at the bottom to place my shoes when I walked in. And on top of the table sat a glass bowl for my keys. The final piece to the puzzle was an off-white chair that was positioned cater-corner to the table and was also my current saving grace, because it gave me the chance to sit and take a breath as I unbuckled the heels from around my ankles and eventually slipped them off my thankful feet.

Now I was really home.

I inhaled deeply and was just about to lean back in the chair and briefly close my eyes when I heard my phone vibrating nonstop in my cross-body purse. I could see the clock on the wall in the living room from where I sat and noticed it was already 10:30 a.m. *Yikes!* I thought. I hadn't realized how much time had gone by since I arrived in London, and I had yet to tell anyone that I made it safely. Before even checking, I knew it was very possible that it was either my friends in DC or my parents in Chicago chastising me.

Unfortunately for me, it was both.

From my parents' text chain:

Mom: You know, I always thought I made a good decision by having just one child, but maybe my second child would know better than to post a photo on Instagram before telling her mother she made it across the world safely.

Dad: That's true, Sharon. A second child would have to know better than to do that to her parents.

Oh boy, here we go, I thought, rolling my eyes. I didn't have the heart to tell them that a second child would have maybe also gotten them off my back sometimes, but it definitely crossed my mind. What also gave me pause was the fact that they were both readily admitting to stalking my Instagram page even though I specifically did not follow them on any social media. This was why I went back and forth with turning my page private and public; clearly it was time to consider putting it on private again.

Hi Mom and Dad! I finally texted back. I'm so sorry.

I was trying to be nice and wait until I figured you would be up before saying anything.

Mom: Robin, now you know you can call us at any time. I'm your mother; I just want to know you're safe.

You're right, Mom. I know. I am sorry. But you saw my post, right? So, you actually did know I was safe. Plus, I literally just walked into my flat maybe five minutes ago, so you're still the first people I'm talking to in the US.

Mom: Okay, my good baby.

I could hear my mom's tone through her texts. She wanted to fuss more but was stopping herself. Clearly, this was where I got my famous snark from.

Mom: I'm glad you're there.

Dad: And she's glad she's first. Don't let her skirt by that part.

Oh, I'm aware, I texted back while laughing. I've been knowing you two for 30 years! I know you well.

Mom: Well, if you know us so well, little girl, you would have sent us that picture first, too.

Yes, ma'am. I will make up for it. As soon as I get settled, I will take plenty of pictures of my apartment and send them to you both first.

Dad: Oh, we'll get to see the pictures before your friends?

Yes, Dad. I promise.

Mom: Don't let her lie to you, Larry, that's just because she's going to Facebook or VideoTime or whatever that thing is called with them instead.

FaceTime, Mom. FaceTime lol

   I couldn't stop smiling as I texted with my parents, still seated in the chair in the hallway. Sure, they could be annoying, like any parents, and their texts certainly had started that way today, but they loved me unde-niably. And my mom also loved being loved, which was why she needed to know I was thinking of her first—and also probably why she was so intent on me finding someone who loved me like my father did her. All that I could understand, but what I could not com-prehend, and what made this whole conversation that much more hilarious, was how Sharon Johnson could be hip enough to know things like how to stalk me on Instagram but could never remember simple stuff like what a popular video app was called.

Okay, speaking of the girls, they are also texting me

nonstop right now. I'm sure I'm about to get in trouble from them, too. Can I call you guys later?

Dad: Of course, sweetheart. We'll be here.

Mom: We love you.

I love you, too.

I clicked right over to the other text chain and saw what felt like eight million texts saying one thing: ROBIN BRIDGET JOHNSON.

It was never a good sign when anyone called me by my full name. It either meant I was in trouble or they were breaking up with me. And here, they were just typing it out over and over again.

Sorry, sorry... I texted back as quickly as my fingers would let me. FaceTime?

I didn't even get a response—just the first video call from Jennifer.

"So, is this like when you went to London before and had a whole secret prince boyfriend for months without telling us?"

As she attempted to put me in the hot seat how only Jennifer could—in a soft voice that let you know she was upset—she also simultaneously let Reagan and Rebecca into the video call.

"No, that's not what happened at all this time," I replied. "I just got caught up and didn't notice the time."

"Mmm-hmm," Reagan responded, jumping right into the conversation as she came onto the screen. Rebecca, meanwhile, was attempting to play silent bad cop by just squinching her eyes toward me like she was a prosecutor waiting for me to divulge a secret.

"I promise, you guys. Seriously. But also, have pity on me. I just got grilled my parents—not by you, too, please," I pleaded into the phone, half jokingly and half not.

"Oh, well, if Mr. and Mrs. Johnson did it already, I guess we can give you a reprieve," Reagan chimed in again.

"Thank you, thank you. Much appreciated."

I nodded my head in gratitude while holding my phone up so that they could see me.

"Only because I'm more than sure that your parents said everything we would have said already," added Jennifer.

"That they definitely did—trust me."

"Well, it's what you get for posting a picture on the 'Gram without—"

"Hey, hey!" I shouted out, interrupting Rebecca before she went any further. "It was just two seconds ago we all agreed I didn't need the repeat. Right? Am I crazy?"

"No, no, you're right," she said, rolling her eyes.

What was it about video that was so much better than phone calls again, I thought to myself as I attempted to ignore her facial expression.

"Well, at least give us the goods on some stuff," Jennifer said, saving the conversation from going into a different direction. "Does the apartment look like it was advertised?"

"Honestly, I haven't even made it past the foyer yet," I said, swinging my phone around so they could see the full, expansive room around me.

"You're telling me that fancy chair you're sitting in right now is only in the foyer?" Reagan asked, her voice going up an octave and giving away her disbelief.

"Indeed. It's pretty comfortable, too."

"That's hella amazing, Rob. I feel like maybe 2 percent of apartments in DC are prefurnished, and likely not with anything as comfy or fancy-looking as that," added Jennifer, her Bay Area accent slightly peeking out due to her excitement.

"Yeah, it's definitely a plus to living in London, that's for sure. But, I mean, I certainly want to add some items that make it feel more like me, too, you know."

"Ha! Is that code for 'it's not going to feel like home until I've added all my Mariah Carey albums to the bookshelf'?" asked Jennifer.

"And, of course, multiple vases full of pink and purple camellias," added Rebecca.

"Oh, maybe not that," Jennifer chimed in. "That might remind her too much of you-know-who."

"Oh right. Damn, I'm sorry," Rebecca said, shrugging.

"But wait, don't forget the cocktail kit so she can make her famous pomegranate-and-prosecco punch topped with pomegranate seeds and mint leaves," said Reagan, interrupting the conversation before it led to Eric.

"Or just a simple rum and Coke!" The three of

them shouted in unison, making fun of my two favorite drinks.

"And anything Chicago, too! I know you brought at least one mug with you that says something about Chi-Town," said Rebecca.

"Yes! Definitely that," Jennifer agreed.

"Are you guys finished or are you done?" I asked after listening to them try to name all the little quirks and knickknacks they thought were important to me.

"Oh, we're done for now, Birdman," Reagan answered, only slightly reassuring me but mostly solidifying the smile on my face that I needed in that moment.

I was already in full on giggle mode when Jennifer busted into a bird call sound to complement Reagan's reference to me as Bryan "Birdman" Williams.

"Did you just make a bird sound?" Rebecca asked in complete disbelief.

We could all tell she was genuinely confused, which only made the cackles from the rest of us grow louder.

"Becs, how is it that some of your closest friends are Black women and you still don't know basic Black pop culture moments?" Reagan asked in between spurts of laughter.

"Okay, but I'm doing better," Rebecca noted. "I know *sooo* much '90s R&B now."

This comment, sincere and ridiculous as it was, only garnered more snickers from all of us on the call, including Rebecca herself. It also reminded me just how much I was going to miss seeing these three at least once a week during our regularly scheduled Nacho

Thursdays—which only occasionally happened on Thursdays.

"So do we get the virtual tour now or are you still recuperating from traveling?" Reagan asked.

"I think I've rested my feet long enough that I can get up—just don't tell my parents. I literally just told them they'd see the place first."

"Your secret is safe with us," Jennifer said, crossing her fingertips in front of her lips as if to zip them closed.

"Yeah, no way I want Mama Johnson mad at me," added Reagan.

Room by room, I walked my best friends through the flat, pointing out little intricacies as I noticed them, like the collection of Jane Austen books on the built-in shelves in the living room or the wicker basket of mini toiletries on the bathroom counter. They each took turns dutifully making ooh and ahh comments, equally participating in my excitement and wonder. As we entered the bedroom, Rebecca practically jumped through the phone when she saw the lavender tufted bed frame and matching trunk in front of it.

"Wow, I can't believe that's real and not just some prop furniture they used to lure you into renting the place," she remarked.

"You thought it was fake?" I asked, recalling all the times I'd showed them the photos of the listing once I finally settled on it.

"I thought it was maybe too good to be true," she admitted. "Only *you* would actually find a purple bed frame in a prefurnished apartment—complete with complementary gray curtains and a crystal-looking lamp on the bedside table. Hello?!"

"She's right, you know," said Jennifer, pausing before she made any further comments to add some drama to the rest of what she was going to direct to me. "Are you *sure* you didn't sneak off to London and decorate this place yourself at some point?"

"I promise you, I did no such thing. Why do you think I'm so sneaky all of a sudden?" I asked, halfway insulted that my best friend in the group kept making little jokes about me secretly doing things in London without her knowledge. Before I could get too upset, however, I reminded myself that we were all trying to adjust to the reality of me moving across the ocean— Jenny probably more than everyone else, since we'd been each other's yin and yang since our first day of college. Almost thirteen years of friendship helped you give people grace and understand when their jokes were probably just a facade for their fears.

"You know what? Don't answer that," I interjected before anyone, especially Jenn, attempted to respond to my very rhetorical question. "Truthfully, I just approached looking for my flat like I tell you guys to treat any kind of shopping—no convincing. I didn't even consider any of the flats that I couldn't answer a resounding yes to when I asked myself if I loved it."

"That's true—you do always say that," Jenn remarked, nodding her head in agreement.

"And I guess it worked for you," added Reagan.

"It always does!" I exclaimed, mentally patting myself on the back for my shopping outlook, which also resonated with every other part of my life. No convincing. I had to know that I loved the job, the apartment, the clothes, the lifestyle, the man…oh wait, there was *one* area of my life where it hadn't quite worked out as well.

"Well, mostly does," I said, correctly myself.

I didn't have to say what the amendment was about. My girls, astute as they were, already knew.

"Speaking of that…" Reagan said in a soft voice that gave away her hesitancy to broach the topic. "Are you hoping to date in London again or is this going to be your 'I'm a boss, independent woman' era?"

"If I'm honest, Rae," I started, "I hope it's neither. Don't get me wrong—I definitely want to make a splash in the new job and take London by storm, kick some investment firm butt over here. But I'm tired of being Miss Independent. I want someone to enjoy this life with. I look at you three and I know things aren't always perfect, but you have partners you can count on. Someone who you know loves you, as you are right now. I want that. And I'm really hoping I don't have to date as many frogs as I did in DC to find him in London."

"Ooh, so you want to have a boo with an accent, huh?" Jennifer asked with a giggle.

"I'll take an accent. As long as he can appreciate a good deep-dish pizza every once in a while—because you know I've already told the Johnsons they have to send me Chicago care packages every few months—makes me laugh, understands my busy life and appreciates me for me, I'm open."

"Aw, that's sweet, Rob," said Jennifer, her smile beaming through the phone.

"He gotta be fine, too, though," said Rae. "You know if you're manifesting and praying on this, we want to be specific!"

"Ha-ha, that's very true. He *does* need to be fine as well."

"And make your insides all gooey."

"What in the world, Becs? What?" I asked, staring at her through the phone.

"You know what I mean. He needs to make you *feeeeeel* all the 'this is the one' feelings."

"I don't know. I feel like I had that with Eric, and it didn't last."

"You're telling me you don't want passion and chemistry? I don't believe you," said Jennifer, asking and answering her own question.

"Of course I want passion. But I want more than that, too. I want something real, something sustainable, something—"

"That you don't have to convince yourself of," added Reagan.

"Yes," I said with a sigh. "I want to just know that he's mine. Is that too unrealistic?"

"Nothing's unrealistic, honey, if you want it bad enough," said Rebecca. "I married a man who was about as monogamous as they come, and now we're both enjoying our very poly lifestyle and thinking of bringing a baby into our world. So, anything is possible. It just might take some time."

"And I don't want it to take a ton of time," I admitted.

"Well, all right then," said Jennifer with an *okay, girl* tone.

"You all said be specific," I reminded them.

"That we did," the three of them responded in unison.

"So, I specifically don't want to go into thirty-one still wondering why love is the only thing I can't seem to get right. And I've got three months to make that happen."

"You got this, Rob. I truly believe the right person is out there for you, and…"

"Jenny, please don't say it's going to happen when you least expect it."

"I wasn't going to say that," she replied, clutching her chest in mock defense. "I know we've all heard that far too many times. I was just going to say that when you do meet him, and I know you will, he's going to be the luckiest guy in London."

"Aw, thanks, bestie," I said, my heart starting to swell up again. "See, this is why I love you. Why I love all of you."

"We love you, too," said Rebecca.

"And I know you probably need to go, but text us when you get settled?" Jennifer asked.

"Of course."

"No matter the time," added Reagan.

"Yes, ma'am."

"And—"

I interrupted Becs before she could say what I knew was on the tip of her tongue.

"And I know, no more Instagram posts before I send it to you all."

"Okay! That's all we're saying," she replied.

We exchanged another round of *I love you*s before finally hanging up the FaceTime call, my apartment suddenly feeling extremely quiet and empty with them no longer virtually with me. If there was one thing I was still worried about, it was whether I'd find any friends in London I could connect with like I did with these women. Not wanting to stay in that feeling too long, I scooped myself off the matching lavender tufted ottoman perfectly placed in front of my new bed and began taking photos for my parents. It was only a matter of time before they texted me asking me where they were, and I wanted to avoid another standoff as much as possible.

Room by room, I retraced my steps with my girls, taking photos of all the little knickknacks we'd identified so I could send those to my parents in addition to the wide shots of the various rooms. I knew my mom was going to get a kick out of the fact that there was a mirror in every room except the kitchen, and my dad was going to love the floor-to-ceiling bay windows in the living room.

It took me about twenty minutes to photograph everything I wanted to send them, and then with the press of a simple send button, my images were off to my parents thousands of miles away. Almost instantly, I heard back from them.

Mom: Robin, it's beautiful.

Dad: Just like my little girl.

Mom: We're so proud of you, sweetheart.

Thanks, guys, I texted back. I can't wait for you to see it in person.

Mom: Neither can we.

I only hoped that by the time they came to visit, I'd also be introducing them to the future Mr. Robin Johnson. That way they could see me have all the things they'd ever wanted for me. All the things I'd wanted, too, truthfully.

Done with all my overseas obligations for the moment, I walked back to the foyer to grab my suitcases and began putting my clothes, shoes, makeup and, yes, my MC albums where I'd need them to be to get through the rest of the week. I had two days left to get settled and then it was go time at work. The next time I walked into those offices, it was going to be as Robin Bridget Johnson, the new head of RFP, marketing and data. And I needed all my ducks in a row to pull off the level of confidence I wanted to exude.

Maybe it was going to be a good thing, after all, that there were so many mirrors in my new flat. No matter which room I left, I'd know one thing for sure. Every inch of me would be perfection when I walked in those doors Wednesday morning.

Chapter Three

At 8:30 a.m. Wednesday morning, I watched as my team piled into the glass-door conference room that I'd asked my assistant to schedule for us. One by one, they walked in, some talking with their colleagues, others still clearly in need of their morning coffee or tea. But each one perked up just a little more upon seeing the spread of muffins, scones and crumpets immaculately set up on the table for our meeting.

From where I positioned myself—standing off to the side, not quite in the corner, but not blocking the main conference table, either—I had a clear view of each individual person's reaction, not only to the setup, but to me. And, of course, there was no way they could miss me, not with my tailored-to-perfection, mono-chromatic burnt orange pantsuit and matching button-down blouse, four-inch nude pointed-toe pumps, and the five-thousand-watt smile plastered on my face.

I waited for each person to find their seat and then finally spoke as I moved toward mine.

"Good morning, team."

Thankfully, I heard a litany of good mornings and hellos in response.

"Most of you already know me and have worked with me for years," I said, carefully sitting down so as not to ruin my vigilantly planned speech. "And I want you to know that even though I'm running the global team now, I am the same person who was here working with you last August. My fundamentals haven't changed—I believe in hard work, compassion among our coworkers, honesty at all times and the power of a bold statement outfit."

With my last few words, I smiled brightly and gestured to my suit, equally trying to lighten the mood in the room and acknowledge, especially for some of the employees I hadn't already worked with, that yes, I understood, I was probably not what they would consider a typical investment firm manager. Not standing five-foot-nine as a Black woman with blond balayage hair, thick thighs and a penchant for statement clothing.

"But as much as I love to have fun, and I want this to be a team that takes the time to enjoy our moments with each other—hello, Nando's Fridays—I am about my business," I continued. "And I need you all to be about yours, too. We have some amazing opportunities coming down the line in the emerging markets, and I want bold ideas from everyone. This is your chance to shine, so please don't hold back. No concept is too much if you've thought it through and you believe it will work."

I paused for a few seconds, like I'd practiced in the mirror the night before, so that I could let everyone process my words fully.

"How does that sound?" I finally asked.

Looking around, I saw several eager eyes staring back at me, and even a few nods and thumbs-up, so I took it all as my cue they were on board.

"Great, so if there are no objections, let's make this a joint get-to-know-me/brainstorming meeting. There are two or three of you who I haven't met yet, but really, it's always great to ask the new boss any questions you have up front, even if you have worked with that person before. So, I'm here, and I'm an open book."

Before I completely finished my speech, I grabbed the nearest scone to me and took a big bite, relaxing my shoulders as I enjoyed the sensation of chewing it. "And please feel free to eat," I said when my mouth was empty again. "We didn't get these scones for them to just look pretty."

With a wink to the table, I took another bite and nodded in the direction of one of the guys who would normally sit right next to me in our row of cubicles when I'd come to visit London. He was the first person who'd messaged me "congratulations" on WhatsApp when he learned I'd campaigned for and gotten the promotion, so I was hoping he was still on my side just a few months later.

"Frank, how about you get us started. Anything on your mind?"

"So much, Robin," he said, shifting in his seat. "First off, I know I said it before, but it's different in person, so I want to give you a proper congratulations. We are really happy for you. You are the perfect person for this job."

"Thank you, Frank. I appreciate that."

And I really did. It's not always easy rising up the ranks in a job with people you've worked with for a while. So, it was nice hearing that there was no resentment among the team—at least no outward expression of it.

"To the business part, I'd love to talk through this new fund we're launching in a few months."

Frank, too, grabbed a muffin from the center of the conference table in a very clear symbol of solidarity.

"Hit me with it," I responded, leaning slightly back into my chair. "What are you thinking in terms of marketing for it?"

"Well, I've been working with the new portfolio manager, Olivia, on this new social impact fund, and we think it's the perfect opportunity for a massive digital campaign to reach the millennial audience—not just your typical website with a logo and a bit of text. We're thinking a fully mobile-optimized website, one with dynamic photos and short videos explaining the content to enhance the user experience and leaning into the idea that they will get a financial and purpose-driven return on their investment."

"And all your plans for this are within US and UK regulations?" I asked.

"Absolutely."

"Okay, let's talk more about this, Frank, but I like it. It's meeting our audience where they are, and I think that's a great idea. Good job."

I paused and looked around the room again.

"Anyone else?"

For the remaining forty minutes of our meeting, I fielded a host of questions ranging from whether orange was my favorite color (*it is not*) to what I thought the most promising markets were going to be in the next few months. It was good to be back in the office again and bonding with my team, and I was excited for what we were going to do going forward. I was also quite curious about this new portfolio manager, Olivia. If she had been the one to inspire Frank to think outside the box, I wanted to meet her as soon as possible.

Two hours after the meeting ended, I made my way to the shared kitchen to pour myself some more coffee. While I'd been working in investment firms since I graduated college, I still never got used to the early morning rise. It normally took me two to three mugs of coffee, especially when I was in London and trying to adjust to the time difference, before I was fully present. So far, on this morning, I'd only had two.

I was hoping to have the room to myself to relax for a bit between the remainder of my morning meetings, but there was one woman already there, presumably hoping for the same. To my pleasant surprise, she was a Black woman—slender, with a glowing skin tone that rivaled the beauty of Adelayo Adedayo, jet-black hair flowing down her back and the most amazing pair of black-and-white-striped sling-back heels with a matching bow on the outside. Before I'd even spoken to her, she reminded me of a combination of myself, Reagan and Jennifer. She was slim with cocoa-brown skin like Jenny, had long hair and a clear penchant for fabulous shoes like Rae and she was frantically but not successfully trying to refill her cup of coffee—a woman after my own heart. The only thing better than having a moment of quiet, I realized, was meeting another Black woman in the office, so I'd take it.

"Hi, I'm Robin," I said, interrupting her attempts with the single-serve coffee machine and stretching my hand out as I walked toward her.

"Oh hello, I'm Olivia," she replied, her British accent pouring out of from her lips. "I've heard so much about you. Ever since I joined, people have been telling me how I *have* to meet you."

"That's so funny—I was just about to say the same thing," I countered. "Frank couldn't stop gushing about working with you this past month."

I silently pushed her mug in the right place for the machine to work and clicked the button for it to begin pouring her coffee, the sweet aroma of French roast filling the room.

"Oh my gosh, thank you," she said, drawing her hands to her chest in gratitude. "And aw, that's really sweet. Frank has been a lifesaver. I've clearly only been here a bit, and he's really helped me as I try to get my sea legs at the new job."

"Yeah, he's good like that. He was the first person to take me to Nando's for Friday lunch when I would come to visit for a couple weeks at a time. He really helped put me at ease in a new country, you know."

"Oh, absolutely. And that's how I've felt joining a new company. I know my work, but learning all the bits and pieces has been challenging sometimes," she said, gesturing toward the coffee machine with a knowing acknowledgment that she was still even learning how to make that work.

With her cup finally full, Olivia moved to the side to let me take my turn at the coffee machine, but I could sense there was more she wanted to say. I let the silence between us linger a bit to give her the opportunity to tell me more.

"It's just that—" she said, hesitating slightly but then ultimately swallowing down her reluctance to speak freely "—as lovely as Frank and everyone else here have been, I'm really happy to meet another young Black woman in the office."

"Now, *that* I completely understand," I responded, dropping my shoulders in relief. I was worried she was about to tell me something horrible about my favorite work peer. Instead, it was just her admission of glee to not be "the only," at least in our part of the firm. I knew the feeling, of course.

"In fact, I wonder if you'd be open to getting a drink together sometime soon?" I asked. "I don't really know a ton of people here except my team, and I could use a friend…and maybe even a wingwoman from London while I try to find my love match in the UK."

Olivia smiled back at me, a smirk building on her face that told me she and I would get along just fine.

"What is it that they say in America?" she asked. "Say less?"

"Ha-ha, yes, that's one of my favorite phrases, too," I replied, recalling my airport buddy who'd just days ago used the phrase in a similar way.

"Perfect. Then, say less, Robin. I'm free tomorrow night, if you are."

"I'm very free," I said, scooping up my mug after hearing the machine stop whirring to indicate that my coffee was ready. "And my friends call me Rob."

"My friends call me Liv," she said, and then looked at the clock on the wall. "Oh, I have to get back to my office, but Rob, I'm so excited we met. And I can't wait until we can talk more tomorrow."

"The feeling is very mutual," I replied.

When Olivia had left the kitchen, I sat down in one of the white chairs, took a big sip of my coffee and immediately pulled out my phone. I had to memorialize this moment in the best way I knew possible, so I went straight to my WhatsApp, found the message chain named Three Rs + a J, and began typing.

I just made a new friend, I texted the girls. And she's a boss Black woman like me J

Reagan: Yay! Our Rob is all grown-up and meeting new people.

Rebecca: We're so happy for you, Robin! Although, it's not like you've ever been shy, so I knew you would.

This is true, but you never know how long it will take to make that kind of connection with someone, I responded. I lucked up by meeting Rae and Jenn the first day of college. And everyone knows those are the people you just kind of have to stay close with; they don't let you leave them.

Jennifer: Whatever, you love us lol. You just make sure she knows you already have a best friend.

Of course! No one could ever replace you, Jenny. Or either of you. But I am really excited now. We're getting drinks tomorrow! And she agreed to being my wingwoman, so maybe this is just the start of my happy texts to the group.

Reagan: Yes! I'm so thrilled for you. I know you were really worried about finding connection there. Definitely keep us updated on know how it goes. Oh, and how's the first day of work as the new boss?

It's going pretty well, actually, I texted back. I really can't complain. My team is great, my outfit is popping, and now I have my first nonwork plans tomorrow. I feel like it's a definite sign of good things to come.

Rebecca: That's so great. Wait, what's our new bestie's name?

It's Olivia, but she told me to call her Liv, I texted back.

Jennifer: Liv! Well, she's already family if we have a nickname.

I know, right?! I responded, deciding it was probably best to leave out the fact that I also told her she could call me Rob. Okay, let me go do some actual work. I just had to let you three know progress was being made.

Rebecca: I love it.

Reagan: Talk soon!

Jennifer: We love you. And oh, send a picture of your outfit.

You got it.

I closed out our text message chain, picked up my mug and headed back to my office. I had the perfect lighting in there to take my photo to send to the group. Plus, I only had twenty more minutes before my next meeting, which was just enough time to begin pulling out all my knickknacks I'd brought to make the office my own.

Chapter Four

"Can I get a spiced apple martini, please?" I asked the bartender at Dirty Martini, handing over my credit card to start a tab for us. We were seated at the high-top bar in the restaurant, which was flanked by a rectangle of sky-blue lights and filled with the finest of liquors in the city. And I, for one, was thrilled that Liv and I had made good on our plans and met up after work to get to know each other better.

"I'll have a blueberry and lavender martini, thanks," she added.

We both turned back to each other, smiling like two high school friends who'd just met.

"Rob, you were telling me how much you love shopping, yes?"

"*Love* might just be an understatement," I said,

laughing. "Shopping and dating were my two favorite pastimes in DC—and they both have at times cost me a lot, one taking all my money and the other all my pride."

"Oh gosh, I remember both of those feelings."

"Thankfully, I've learned how to balance my expensive tastes with some trendy, cheaper items. Even here, I used to only go to Harrods and Harvey Nichols, but then some kind soul put me onto Primark."

"Yes! Oh, I love Primark. I'm glad you know about it. Once I moved to The City from Brixton, I had to literally tear myself away from going every weekend. Now I just go if I know I have a holiday coming up."

"Ooh, that's a good idea. I'm already realizing there are pros and cons to learning about this gem of a store—but yes, it was one of my first very grateful London finds."

"Well, I have to tell you. You're quickly becoming one of mine! Obviously, I have my close friends from school, but finding a friend in our investment firm who just so happens to love Primark, fancy drinks and caffeine drips in the morning... I'm over the moon!"

"Very same, Liv," I said, winking at her. "And I hope you know that I'm here for whatever you need at the job. I may not be a London expert, but I know these folks, and I want to make sure we both succeed."

The bartender slid our drinks to us, and without a word, we both delicately raised our glasses for a toast.

"Cheers to us," I said.

"Cheers to new friends."

"Yes, absolutely."

I took a sip and closed my eyes at how good it tasted. The way the gin, apple flavoring, liqueur and bitters were mixed together was enticingly perfect.

"Now I just need to find a London bae, and I'll be all set."

"Okay, yes, tell me more about this quest for love, please, because I'm having a hard time understanding how *you* are single."

"It's a tale as old as time, my dear Olivia."

"But you're fabulous! I thought the way people spoke about you before you ever even came back told me everything I needed to know, and then I met you, and somehow you were even more gorgeous, more poised and more put together than I ever expected."

"Wait, don't make me cry here. I don't have on waterproof mascara," I said, laughing.

"Sorry!"

"But no, honestly, that's really sweet, especially coming from the woman sitting before me whose skin literally glows in sunlight."

"*Nooo,*" Liv protested, her British accent growing stronger with every sip of her drink.

I looked at her over my glass as if to say, *take the compliment*, and she stopped herself from objecting further.

"Well, thank you," she said, her rosy undertones peeking through on her cheeks. "But we were talking about you. How has no man, or woman—I don't want to assume—scooped you up yet?"

"That's a great question, Liv. And I have, like, so many answers and also none."

I took a gulp of my drink, realizing I needed something to help me get through my sad story that I was about to detail to this woman who'd all but told me that she'd considered me an urban legend before she met me. Who knew what she would think after I spilled all my tea?

"The thing is, I've always considered myself a woman who goes after what she wants and gets it. I know that sounds kind of pretentious, but it's true. I've worked hard to make sure I've gotten everything I want in life—from the job I busted my tail to prove I deserved to the life I've cultivated that's filled with things like trips to sixty-plus countries, designer clothes (but only the ones that look good, because we know they all don't), friends that I can call at any moment who will stop what they are doing for me and more. But when it comes to men—and yes, thank you for not assuming, but it is men—there's just been this ceiling that I can't seem to break."

"Robin, I'm so sorry. Not to try to simplify things too much, but do you think it's the kind of men you're dating? Maybe they are intimidated by you," Liv asked, sitting up straight in her seat, completely listening intently as I spoke.

"I've dated *a lot*, though. So even if it was occasionally that for some reason the guy making six figures was intimated by me trying to do my best out here, that's not the whole story. Honestly, I could fill a football stadium with the litany of reasons it hasn't worked out. In fact, you name it and it's probably happened to me. I had one guy ghost me after dating for two years.

Another guy cheated on me, but he was so bad at it that I found out because he called me the other girl's name one time. I've had more than one man stand me up, but the most memorable one happened on Valentine's Day a few years ago, when I was literally sitting in the middle of this all-you-can-eat steak house in DC waiting for hours for a dude who never showed up, never called or texted, nothing. And it had been his idea!

"Last year, I was in a fairly serious long-distance relationship with this guy here in London. That one started off perfect. He was super romantic, and I think he genuinely adored me, but at some point, I realized we were too different for it to succeed. And so, after yet another heartbreaking end, I decided to form a dating pact with one of my friends to try to get over him. We both went on a date with at least one guy a week for a few months. And you know what happened? The pact ended when she reconnected with her ex, and I... just got tired of dating a bunch of guys who were never going to really be the one."

"Wow, I can understand how all of that probably feels incredibly defeating."

"That's a good word to describe it, because it's not that I haven't put in the effort. It just hasn't materialized into something long-standing for me. And then well-meaning people—thankfully none of my close friends, but others—will contradict themselves and say things like, 'Well, it'll happen when you least expect it, Robin,' or better yet, 'You just have to treat it like you do your career. You don't give up when one thing doesn't go according to your plans with that, so you can't do it with dating, either.' And I get where they're coming from, but they don't seem to understand how exhausting it is to try over and over again and feel like a failure at it each time. Especially when I don't fail. Like, that's just not a thing I do."

I suddenly realized I'd delved into a monologue again in London, this time with Olivia, and we'd only known each other for a few days. I hoped she didn't immediately think I was a stuck-up, selfish person who deserved to never find love.

"I'm sorry, I didn't mean to drone on that long," I said before taking another sip to try to drown my awkwardness.

"Please don't apologize. I know exactly how you feel. I never did a dating pact," she said. "But I tried a lot of frogs before meeting my prince, and I hated all the things that people said to me before we met, too."

"OMG," I squealed with glee at yet another connection between us. "I just said that same frogs-and-prince phrase to my friends the other day."

I decided it was best to leave out the fact that I'd actually dated a real prince, and even that hadn't worked out.

"Of course you did! We're the British and American versions of each other," Olivia replied. "The only difference is that I'm four years older than you, so maybe that can give you some slice of hope. David and I only met two years ago, which means you're no worse off than I was when I was thirty."

"Well, British version, please tell me, how did you finally meet your prince?"

"To be honest, it was not easy… I probably didn't date as much as you, but I had some of the same crushing thoughts, because it just seemed like nothing ever worked. But then one day, I met David like so many people here meet their significant other—he was a friend of a friend who I met at a get-together."

"Ugh, that sounds very similar to America."

"One thing that's a little different, at least from what I see on TV, is that the men here are not very straight-forward. I don't know if you're used to that or not, but I wouldn't rely on it here, even at things like a get-together, although that can often be your best bet. It's just so rare that I ever had a guy stop me on the street to ask for my number or anything of the sort, so really, I lucked up. I know that's not at all helpful."

"No, it is! Any insight into the British dating scene is useful right now."

"Well, you should also know that British men are notoriously cheap," Liv said, her eyes growing wide to emphasize her point. "I had one friend go on a date with a guy who counted up what he spent and she spent, and then he tried to charge her for her amount later that evening."

"After a first date?!" I asked, incredulous.

"After a first date."

"Oh my."

I took another two sips of my drink as I took in these new revelations, realizing at the same time that I'd almost finished my glass.

"Does that mean you have someone in mind you can introduce me to, then? I take setups."

"Ha-ha—it's funny you ask that. When we first met and you mentioned needing a wingwoman, I thought about my younger brother for you. He's a photographer, and he and his girlfriend just broke up a couple months ago."

"Tell me more," I said leaning in closer to her.

"But…then I figured it probably wouldn't be a good idea. As much as I love Craig, and you'd likely find him very charming, he's just not the best at communicating with his girlfriends. It's what messed up his last relationship. And I really don't want to ruin this newfound friendship we have because he decides to be an idiot with you."

"That's very fair. I'm sure Craig is a catch, but I can't handle yet another guy who finds honest communication scarier than your basic horror movie. I've had too much therapy to settle for that again."

"I completely understand…oh, speaking of therapists, do you have one in the UK already?"

"No, not yet. So if you have someone you can recommend, I'd love that."

"I have a few people I can connect you with, actually."

"Perfect. What about churches?"

"I can come up with a list of those, too!"

"Move over, Frank. You, Liv, might be the real lifesaver."

I took the last sip of my drink and motioned for our bartender so that we could place another drink order.

"What would you like?" she asked as she walked over to us.

"I think I'm going to try the wild strawberry martini this time," I responded and then turned to Liv to see if she wanted another drink, too.

"I'll get the passion fruit martini," Liv added.

"Excellent choices," said the bartender, turning back to the lit-up shelving to get the liquors and accoutrements for our drinks.

"I'm going to take this opportunity to find the loo," I said, winking to Liv and trying my best at a London accent.

"Ha-ha. You can also say restroom," she responded, laughing and returning my signature wink.

"Okay, off to the restroom loo I go!"

I nearly jumped off my high chair, instantly happy that I'd worn my most comfortable heels—a pair of white satin, vintage-inspired Jimmy Choos covered in faux pearls—since I suddenly needed to run toward the bathroom as fast as I could. While they looked incredibly elegant and sophisticated, especially paired with my off-white blazer, cream boat-neck blouse and navy blue pants, they had magic-level cushions inside them that felt like pillows cuddling my feet. This fact came in handy as I beelined to my destination, running so fast that I almost crashed into a beautiful British man with stunning hazel eyes on my way there.

"So sorry," I shouted out and kept running.

"Quite all right," I heard him say behind me as the restroom door closed.

Coming back out of the restroom, I noticed that our drinks had already been placed in front of Liv at the bar. But I also observed that a certain handsome Brit was still standing at the spot where I almost ran him over like a semitruck, his slim-fit plaid pants only slightly taking away attention from his broad shoulders and smooth brown skin. And miracle of all miracles, unless I'd completely lost my touch at discernment, he seemed to be waiting for me.

I slowly walked toward him, not yet wanting to let on to the fact that I hoped he would stop me from passing him.

"Hello," he said as I got close enough for his deep but soft voice to reach me.

"Hi," I responded, attempting not to grin like a Cheshire cat. This was exactly the win I needed tonight, so I didn't want to mess things up by coming off too eager.

"I saw you earlier and noticed your American accent."

Oh, right, I thought. I'd quickly forgotten that that I was the one with a different accent where I lived now. While I didn't love being sized up that easily from two words while running past someone, it seemed to have worked in my favor enough to get him to pay attention to me, so plus one for being American, I supposed.

"I am American," I said, stepping closer to him. "I just moved here last week."

"For work?" His eyes peered deeply into mine, nearly causing me to lose my breath for a moment.

"Ahem, yes, for work," I answered, clearing my throat and attempting to steady my heartbeat at the same time. Now positioned directly in front of him, I could just catch a small whiff of his cologne and had to keep myself from closing my eyes and taking in the deepest of breaths in an effort to keep his scent with me when I would inevitably walk back to my seat. "My coworker over there, she brought me out for my first night out as an official Londoner," I said while pointing toward Liv.

"Wicked. Would it be too forward if I asked to take you out for your second night out, then?"

"Absolutely, not. I'd really like that," I said. "But first, maybe we can start with you telling me your name?"

"Oh, I'm so sorry, you're right," he said, drawing his hand to his head in embarrassment. "I don't usually approach women in bars, so I'm a little out of practice."

"It's okay. You're cute enough to make up for such a small blunder," I said jokingly. "I'm Robin, by the way."

I stretched out my hand to his, which he took gently and smoothly, turning it up toward his face before grazing it slightly across his full lips. It was very possibly the first time anyone had kissed my hand before telling me his name, but for some reason, it sent small shivers down my spine.

"I'm Daniel," he said, eventually releasing my hand and returning it back to its completely flummoxed owner.

"Hi, Daniel."

I stared directly into his eyes, not wanting to break the trance just yet, but somewhere deep inside realizing I'd left my newfound friend at the bar long enough.

"Robin, it's a pleasure meeting you," he said, his smile growing wider and wider as we both struggled to take our eyes off the other.

After we exchanged numbers and tentative plans for Saturday, we said our goodbyes so that I could get back to Liv and my wild strawberry martini that I hoped was still chilled. I could practically feel myself wanting to skip back toward her, but I steadied my pace and walked away calmly, also sensing Daniel's eyes on me my whole strut back.

For her part, Liv was just as excited about the developments as I was, as she eagerly waited for the details.

"Robin!" she exclaimed as soon as I sat down.

"I know, right?"

"How cute is he?"

"So cute," I said, grabbing my drink and taking a huge gulp before we dug in further.

"And he came up to you?" she asked.

"Well, yes and no. I kind of ran into him first, but he was the one who asked me out."

"Wow, well, color me pleasantly surprised. Maybe it's the fresh American smell," she added, raising her glass to meet mine for a clink.

"And honestly, if it is, then cheers to being American," I said, bringing my glass to meet hers. "I'll take all the help I can get for now. I'm just sorry I left you sitting here so long."

"Oh, I was fine. And on the bright side, I had time to write down those two lists for you."

Liv slid a white napkin my way with four therapists

and numbers on one side and three church names and locations on the other.

"You're literally an angel," I said to her, placing the napkin in my purse for safekeeping.

"Hopefully an angel and a great wingwoman, because my goal is to make sure you get all that you need while here."

"If that's the case, then I just have one more request."

"Anything," she said, looking at me seriously waiting for what I'd ask next.

"Include me in your friends list for Glastonbury? I know the tickets are hard to get, and they'll be coming out soon and I do *not* want to be stuck out here trying to score some on my own."

"Say less, Rob," she responded with a smile. "That's not even a request from me. My friends and I have scored tickets the past four years, and you're going to have a blast."

Chapter Five

My heartbeat picked up speed as I walked into the Melody at St Paul's—a private dining room situated inside the redbrick, Victorian-style boutique hotel—to meet Daniel for afternoon tea. After I'd explained to him that my favorite activity on a Saturday was getting afternoon tea at Harrods, he was intent on showing me another option—a better option, according to him—that was only thirty minutes away from my flat on the Tube.

Of course, Harrods was only twenty minutes away from me on the Tube and nine minutes by black cab, but I didn't want to press the issue. I was just happy (and nervous!) that a beautiful man had planned out a date for us when I'd only been in London for less than a week. All signs were pointing positively to me being in a relationship by thirty-one.

What was an even better sign was seeing Daniel standing off to the left side of the door, waiting for me with that gorgeous smile of his that stretched fully across his face even as I walked in about two minutes late. His navy blue double-breasted peacoat was unbuttoned and open enough to let his tailored gray shirt peek out from underneath it, and he'd coupled that with a pair of light blue trousers that cupped his legs perfectly and did nothing to hide his excitement to see me.

"Sorry I'm a little late," I said sheepishly, trying not to stare too long.

"It's quite all right, love. You're here now."

I caught his eyes give me a once-over, starting from the tip of my wand-curled hair down to the black-and-white pointed-toe slides I had on my feet. Even with my coat on, I could make out my figure underneath, a fact that was confirmed when his eyes lingered on my charcoal-gray pants and, more importantly, my thighs that they were attempting to cover. With a final glance back up to my face, he gently but with authority took my hand in his and walked us into the restaurant.

Daniel was right that the place was beautiful, with its earth tones of blush pink and sage green mixing with the whites of the tablecloths on the light wooden tables and the gold chandeliers floating from the ceiling. If I were decorating it, I might have wanted to throw in a bold-colored chair or two to spice up the atmosphere, but I understood the look they were going for—pristine, relaxing, sophisticated and muted. The purples, hot pinks and burnt oranges that I loved had no place here.

We were seated almost immediately at a table for two next to the windows that overlooked the stunningly green garden on the interior of the property. Daniel, ever the quintessential British gentleman, pulled out the chair for me to sit down while somehow keeping his magnetic hazel eyes locked on me the whole time. I was thankful we'd spoken on the phone the night prior, or I was pretty certain that his deep, intense stares would have removed any bit of composure that I had in the moment.

As it was, I still found myself concentrating on his lips as he eloquently explained to the waiter that we wanted to partake in the menu option for afternoon tea—complete with sandwiches, scones and preserves—and free-flowing champagne for two hours. I also watched as his chest slowly moved up and down and caught the edge of a hidden tattoo on his left arm peeking out of his rolled-up sleeve. To say I was enamored would have been an understatement.

Once Daniel was done ordering our meal, he turned back to me with his full attention directed my way. It was hard to explain, but he was clearly one of those men who made you both crave to be the focus of his desire and feel instantly undressed when it happened. His eyes had a way of focusing a spotlight on any place or person he looked.

"You seem to have a bit on your mind, Robin," he said. "I've only known you for a couple days, but I don't gather you're a person who sits quietly for very long."

I laughed, loudly, but then was keenly aware that my voice seemed to echo in the quiet restaurant over the soft music playing in the background.

"I am not," I responded. "But I was enjoying watching you just now. I guess it maybe put me in a trance."

"Oh?" he asked, leaning in a little closer to me. "Tell me more," he whispered.

"Well, for example, I noticed this guy desperately trying to show himself." I moved my hand to his left arm and circled the area where I saw the dark black lines jutting out just slightly beyond his sleeve.

"My tattoo? That's what you noticed?"

"One of many things, yes."

He pulled his sleeve up to show me it to me in full—two bands wrapping around his lower arm, the one on top about two inches wide and the bottom one maybe about a half an inch.

"I got it when I was at university," he said. "It's meant to symbolize strength."

"Did it hurt?"

"Quite a bit, yes," he responded with a small chuckle.

"Do you have any others?" I asked.

"Just the one. I thought about getting more, but I already have to cover this one up for work, so I didn't want to have to think about it for more than one."

"That makes sense. If it's any consolation, it looks very sexy on you."

"That is quite the consolation, yes," he said, smiling back at me again. "And you? Do you have any tattoos?"

"I do, but also just the one."

"Show me," he said, subtly licking his lips.

"Sadly, I can't in this fine establishment. But I can tell you that it's a vine of magnolia flowers on my rib cage, right under my breasts."

"I was somehow not expecting that," he said, sitting back into his chair. "You are a wonder, Ms. Johnson."

"I got it after one of my best friends died. She was from Louisiana, and that's their state flower. Plus, it symbolizes purity and endurance. She was one of the purest souls I know, and her death rocked the people she loved pretty hard. I needed something to keep me going after she succumbed to her illness, so I figured why not get a tattoo?"

"I'm so sorry, Robin. I didn't mean to bring up something so terrible."

He leaned in close to me again, but this time with compassion instead of sex appeal. In one sense, I deeply appreciated it, but in another sense, I wanted to make sure that our date didn't devolve into me ugly crying over Christine.

"You couldn't have known—it's okay," I said, attempting to assure him that we could go back to being flirty. "Honestly, it's good to talk about her sometimes, but I'd rather avoid smearing my makeup at the beginning of our first date."

"As you say, very fair."

Thankfully, just then our waiter came back with our serving tray of goodies, two mugs for our tea and two glasses of champagne. The tray featured a litany of desserts at the top, including what looked like the tastiest macaroons; the middle tier held the scones and preserves, and the bottom tier was filled with egg salad, cucumber and salmon sandwiches. As the waiter expertly arranged the items on the table, Daniel grabbed my hand and stroked the inside of my palm with his thumb. It was a quiet gesture, but it helped center us both right back into the date.

"Okay, I don't know about you, but I plan to partake in as much of this champagne as I can in the next two hours," I said as soon as the waiter walked away.

"I'm in full agreement," said Daniel, raising his glass with the hand that wasn't still holding on to mine. "Why do you think I picked this place?"

"Ooh, let me find out my charming Brit has a little devilish side," I said winking to him.

"We all have a little bit of both, don't we, Robin?" he asked, staring deeply into my eyes again.

"Cheers to that."

I met his glass with mine with a delicate clink.

"Most American women do like a guy who can, as they say, rock an impeccably tailored suit and some gray sweatpants equally comfortably."

"Hmm, is this your way of telling me you want to see if I have sweatpants in my wardrobe," he asked, mimicking my wink back to me.

"It's not *not* my way of saying that," I admitted.

"Slow down, Robin," Daniel responded jokingly. "The date's only begun, and I want to make you ask for it before the night's over."

Five hours later, the two of us, tipsy off bottomless champagne pours, were making our way through the numerous bars in Islington. What had started as a harmless statement by Daniel, admitting that he wasn't ready to end the date yet, had turned into a masterful plan for him to show me around a part of the city known for its party scene on a Saturday night. And truthfully, we were having a blast on what ended up being a full day-long date, laughing about everything from our first impressions of each other to our recountings of our worst dates while practically skipping, one of his hands just brushing the small of my back, going to bar after bar. First, we started with the famous Through the Looking Glass cocktail at Little Bat—an *Alice in Wonderland*–inspired drink that mixed together gin, elderflower cordial, lemon sherbet and tonic. Then, we moved on to trying the Ginny in a Bubble and Kiss It Better cocktails (plus a few shots) at Barrio Angel. And now we were seated at the bar at Laki Kane—a pan-Asian restaurant known for its tropical cocktails—and waiting on our drinks as we continued peppering each other with questions and observations.

Daniel ordered a Banana Republic, which was their take on an old-fashioned with whiskey, cognac, wine, sour orange, cane sugar and sun-dried bananas stirred together and served over an ice block. I'd chosen the Beach Coco Cumber—a mixture of spiced dry rum, honey, pineapple, coconut water, fresh mint and cucumber—and an order of prawn fried rice to soak up all the liquor we'd been taking in since 3:00 p.m.

"So, as a Black woman from Chicago, do you miss Barack Obama being president even more than the rest?" Daniel asked me right after we'd just finished talking about things we liked to do as kids. I'd said going to the Chicago Children's Museum with my parents and looking out on Lake Michigan after, which I guess led him to the Obama question. For me, it just produced yet another loud laugh from the depths of my diaphragm, but at least this time I was in an appropriate venue for my outburst.

"What does me being from Chicago have to do with anything?" I asked through tears of laughter.

"He's from Chicago, innit?"

"Well, technically he lived there awhile and considers it home, but that doesn't mean I know him intimately or anything like that to miss him more than anyone else. You don't think all the Black people in Chicago know each other, right?"

"No, but I thought maybe you felt a special connection to him when he was president."

"I think almost every Black person in the United States had that connection. Even the ones who didn't agree with him politically—it was just amazing to see that kind of thing finally happen in real life. I certainly didn't believe I'd ever see a Black man become president, that's for sure."

"We were in awe over here, too."

"I think a lot of people were. But, for me, that had nothing to do with him considering Chicago a second home… I will tell you a secret, though," I said, leaning in close to him as if I was going to reveal something only his ears could hear.

Daniel immediately perked back up after looking

slightly defeated by my earlier statements. I guessed he was ready to hear some scandalous American tale.

"I tried driving past the street where their house was on the South Side of Chicago one time. I saw that it was blocked off by the Secret Service and hurried away as fast as I could. I was so scared they were going to take down my license plate and look me up to see why I was over there when I didn't belong!"

"And did anything happen?" Daniel asked, completely intrigued by my story.

"Not a thing. But I still never went back. I was shook."

"I wouldn't have, either. But you? You're so bloody brave and fierce and funny. I could see you finding your way back there."

"No, really, I'm so very good. If I do happen to meet one of the Obamas one day, it'll be like a normal person at an event or something, not looking like a stalker trying to see their home. That was a dumb idea, to be honest."

"Yeah," said Daniel. "But you have—what do you all call it—cojones? I like that about you. I like for my girlfriend to be bloody brave."

As he spoke more, I noticed that Daniel's once-charming eyes were now glassy, and his speech was beginning to slur. Maybe it was also his now-constant insistence on my bravery or the fact that he'd slipped in the word *girlfriend* on our first date, but I could sense that he was on the verge of embarrassingly drunk. The fried rice couldn't get here soon enough.

"Wow, your American slang knowledge is quite

impressive," I said, jokingly. "But more importantly, girlfriend?"

I attempted to give Daniel my best flirty, but also *I think you might be really drunk and saying things you don't mean* eyes.

"You know that you want me to be your girlfriend already?" I asked.

"I know I want you to be even more than that," he answered quickly, his voice quivering as he scooped up his drink for another gulp as soon as the bartender put it down in front of us.

"I'm sorry, what? What does that mean?"

Suddenly, I realized I couldn't joke my way out of this conversation any longer. We'd barely known each other two days, so while I found Daniel to be very handsome and a ton of fun, I wasn't thinking marriage already. I needed him to fully understand that point. Unfortunately, with a belly full of liquor and only tea sandwiches and scones to help suppress his urges, I could—very disappointingly—tell that Daniel did not. Instead, it seemed that he took my questioning as a sign that I was asking him to proclaim his love for me further. At least that's the only explanation I could come up with as I, shocked, watched him stand up and command attention from everyone in the room.

"Ladies and gentlemen, I apologize for the interruption," he said, his glass still in his hand. "But I must tell you how much this woman here—this *American* woman—has stolen my heart. She doesn't know it yet, but she's going to be my wife."

Even though Daniel had loudly projected to the restaurant the rest of his statement, something inside him must have told him to whisper "wife." But even after he did so, he looked over at me with a huge grin on his face, and I could only stare back in shock, my eyes wide with embarrassment—silently pleading with him to sit back down so that we could resume our very pleasant, very *private* conversation.

"Oops, I guess she knows now," he slurred out, turning back to his new audience and once again missing my cues. Filled with drunk confidence, Daniel walked toward the center of the restaurant to continue his spectacle, almost tripping over his own feet as he maneuvered to the spot he had in mind. "But that's okay. That's okay. I don't deny it," he said aloud. "Who among us isn't ashamed to say we believe in love at first sight?"

I watched as Daniel scanned the crowd looking for validation and then shrank in horror when, one by one, I heard him start to get it.

"I do," shouted one woman.

"Proclaim your love, ol' chap," said a guy at a table on what looked to be a date with two women.

"Cheers," came a voice from far away, prompting multiple people—including Daniel—to raise their glasses in the air.

"Cheers!" he responded back. "Cheers to love!"

I felt like the only person in the room no longer in a jovial mood. Instead of joining into the commotion, I gratefully noticed the bartender place the food near me, turned my body back toward the bar and began trying to shovel forkfuls of rice into my mouth, hoping it would help me feel less humiliated if I just ignored what was happening around me. In truth, if there had been a hole in the bar that could have transported me directly back to Westminster, I would have gladly jumped in it. There was not.

As the moment began dying down, I looked out of my periphery and saw the look on Daniel's face. It was of a man who was finally realizing that his declaration of love on a first date might have been too much, too soon. He thanked the crowd and walked back to his chair, then scooched it closer to mine in an attempt to try to reconnect as he sat down.

"Robin, are you all right?" he asked, his hot, drunk breath now sending chills down my spine in all the bad ways.

"I think you need this rice as much as I do," I responded, pushing my plate over to him and requesting an extra fork from the bartender.

"Uh-oh, you're mad at me. I can tell."

Daniel sat back in his chair and looked at me with the eyes I'd once thought were entrancing. Now, they just seemed utterly sad, like he knew he'd messed everything up. He took the fork from the bartender and ate a few bites of the rice before trying to speak again.

"I went too far," he said, his head lowered.

"It was a lot," I admitted. "I think maybe we had too much to drink with not enough food."

"Yeah, you're right." He paused for a second and then asked the question I could tell he'd been avoiding for the past couple minutes. "Do you want me to take you home?"

"No, thanks. I… I'm just going to catch a black cab and head back on my own. I appreciate the offer, though."

A small tear slid down Daniel's face as I could tell he realized the date was over. One part of me felt really bad, because I couldn't let the spectacle of what had just happened go despite how good a time we'd had the rest of the day. The other part of me remembered my motto—no convincing. It wasn't that I thought he was a bad guy. It was just that I'd seen what I needed to see to show me that we weren't right for each other. I mean, if he couldn't control himself on a first date after a few drinks, how could I believe he'd handle the situation correctly if we were out with my coworkers— or, God forbid, my boss? It also wasn't lost on me that he kept referring to me being American. I got it, of course—there was a desire on both our parts to learn more about each other's cultures, but it was starting to feel icky whenever he brought it up. Like my nationality was a trophy in his eyes. Neither of those things would work for me.

"Okay," he said, resigned to the fact that he wasn't going to change my mind. "Let me pay and at least walk you out."

"That would be nice," I said.

On our way out of the restaurant, with Daniel still positioning his hand on my waist, almost as a subtle reminder to how we'd felt just an hour before, a lady at a corner table shouted, "To love at first sight!" and raised her glass toward us.

"Thank you," we said in soft unison, both of us likely understanding the irony of the moment.

Once outside, it didn't take long for him to hail me a cab. And to his credit, Daniel politely opened my door, helped me inside and gently closed it, despite likely knowing it was the last time we would see each other. As the car drove off, I waved goodbye to him and pulled out my phone from my purse, quickly scrolling to and then opening up my photo gallery. I had one meme in mind that would perfectly sum up the day and my time with Daniel Adjaye for my friends back home.

I met a guy. 2 days later...never mind.

I clicked on the image and shared it to my Three Rs + a J chat with no comment.

Reagan was the first to respond.

Damn, Daniel!

Jennifer: I'm so sorry, Rob. So, I guess that means the date didn't go well?

It was perfect for several hours, I replied. And then, like a faulty roller-coaster ride, it crashed at the end.

Rebecca: Ugh.

Jennifer: We were rooting for you, Daniel. We were all rooting for you!

I knoooow, right?

For the next few minutes, I typed out all my frustrations and a full breakdown of what happened on our date, fully expecting my friends to continue being enraged along with me. When I was met with three notices of them typing and then silence, I realized I wasn't going to get the reaction I'd assumed.

Rebecca was the first person to press Send on her thoughts.

Well, I can see how that was embarrassing, Rob. But was it deal breaker bad?

Yes, it was, I replied swiftly.
Then came Jennifer's text.

Are you sure? Because it seems like you both really liked each other, and he just made an honest mistake after lots and lots of drinks.

I rolled my eyes and sat up straight in the cab. What I needed right now was my friends' support and the beautiful feeling of us coming together to hate a guy I'd been on a bad date with. We'd done this so many times before that I wasn't sure why there was suddenly a difference.

Are you all serious right now? First, you know my motto. But second, how is it that he gets to be sloshy drunk and that's okay? I had just as many drinks as he did, but I wasn't drunkenly declaring my love for him in a restaurant full of strangers...and if I had, he would have likely gone home and told his friends that I was cuckoo for cocoa puffs.

Reagan: No, that's true. You're right. I didn't think of it like that.

I mean...yeah, Rae, c'mon. I'm not unreasonable. But I have standards; I don't think there's anything wrong with that.

Jennifer: There's absolutely nothing wrong with that. You keep us all together, you know that. I guess I'm just worried that your "no convincing" motto will have you miss out on things because you're treating men like a pair of jeans. This guy isn't the guy. We get that. But you do have to allow for people to make some mistakes.

I hear you, I replied, genuinely listening to their feedback. And it wasn't that I didn't agree, but I also knew that giving people too many chances had always set me up for failure in the past. I had to go with my gut, and my gut was throwing out a clear red flag on Daniel.

But this wasn't that, I texted, continuing my thought. Sure, he embarrassed me, but this was also about trust, really. If I can't trust you not to make a fool of us after a few drinks...

Rebecca: That's fair. We get it, and we're totally on your side. Always.

Reagan: Exactly. We just know you wouldn't take any excuses or crap from us, so sometimes we have to turn it back on the master to make sure she's good, too.

Yeah, yeah. I'd much rather be on the other end, I texted back, my mood finally starting to change into something more positive.

Anyway, I'll tell you all more later. I just needed to get that one thing out.

Reagan: We understand, and don't forget, we got you.

Are you back at your apartment?

I'm on my way now.

Jennifer: Okay, well, let us know when you're in safely. Sounds like we need a Nacho Zoom night soon.

I would really love that, I texted back. And I'll be sure to tell you when I walk through my door.

I sat back into my seat and watched the city from my cab window as we drove past the River Thames and headed back to Westminster. All I could think of was how things had gone so horribly wrong so quickly. But after a few minutes, I took in a deep breath and reminded myself that one bad date didn't mean my prospects were over already. As my girls had inadvertently reminded me, I'd been through worse dates, and I wasn't a person who took crap—from people or life—lightly. So, the show was going to go on. I'd only been in London a week, after all. And I wasn't giving up that easily.

Chapter Six

"Rob, you have time?" Olivia said, poking her head into my office.

"Of course, come on in."

I motioned for her to have a seat in one of the two chairs facing my desk and picked up my mug of coffee as she plopped down.

"Second or third cup?" she asked.

"Just second so far."

I briefly glanced at the clock on my wall. It was 11:00 a.m., so I was doing pretty well only being on the second cup. I guess my body was finally starting to adjust to London time.

"I'm glad you stopped by," I said after another sip. "I heard from Frank that the website development for that new fund is going really well."

"Oh, it really is. I've been very impressed by the mock-ups we've seen so far."

"Good! I'm hoping this can be an example of the way we want to continue to partner with the portfolio management team. You guys are the experts on the trends of the market and the investments, and if we listen to you, we can really make magic happen on our side. I'm seeing some great RFPs come across my desk in the past couple weeks, which just gets me really excited for the future."

"Honestly, I'm pretty excited, too. I can feel the shift in our work. It's not revolutionary, but it's just enough to see some big changes happen."

"Yes! I completely agree."

I raised my hand so we could high-five each other across my desk and was happy to see Liv's hand meet mine. *Phew*, I thought. That would have been an embarrassing mishap had she not known that nonverbal cue.

"But…" she said, leaning back into her chair. "I didn't come here to talk work."

"No?" I asked, feigning ignorance.

"You know I want to know how things are going with Mr. Hazel Eyes!" she said, laughing.

"Ugh, crash and burn, girl."

"Oh no!"

"I know. It just ultimately turned out to be too good to be true."

"I should have known when he approached you at Dirty Martini. I don't know a lot of British men who do that, so I have to tell you, my alarms went up. But then I was so excited for you and thought maybe I was wrong."

She shrugged in defeat.

"You were not. I just wish you would have said something then, girl. But it's okay—live and learn."

"I hope that doesn't mean you're giving up."

"Quite the opposite. Last night, I stopped fighting the universe and joined a dating app."

Olivia's eyes widened with excitement.

"Wow, I'm impressed," she said.

"Because I joined a dating app? In America, that's nothing to be impressed about, I can tell you that."

"No, I just mean how quickly you picked yourself up from the last disappointment."

"To be fair," I said, now leaning back in my chair as well, "it was just one date, albeit an incredibly humiliating one. But I didn't need to get over him or anything like that. Plus, I don't have time to waste if I really want to meet this goal by thirty-one."

"Oh yes, how could I forget this goal of yours," she mockingly asked. "Okay, well, you have to let me know how it goes on the app."

"I definitely plan to. I matched with this one cute guy this morning, so I'm hoping he'll say something to me today."

"Ooh, I like it," she said, excitedly moving her fingertips in anticipation. "I have a few mates who have found partners on apps, but not many. I'm hoping it goes better for you."

"Yes, let's hope. And in any case, I expect it to be more as a supplement to meeting guys in person than as my only way. I still need you as my wingwoman for now."

"Reporting for duty, as always. In fact, some of my best girlfriends were going to join us for drinks later this week, if that's all right."

"That's perfect. I can't wait to meet them."

"Excellent!"

Olivia looked down at her phone to check the time.

"Oh, bugger. I'm off to my next meeting, but it was good catching up for a bit."

"Yes, it really was. Maybe next time, I'll stop by your desk for a coffee chat."

"Please don't," she said as she stood up and began walking to my door. "I need this fifteen-minute break away from portfolio land. I'll just come to you."

"Or there's always the kitchen."

"That, too," she said with a wink and then bounced out just as seamlessly as she'd walked in. "Cheers! Talk soon."

At around 7:30 p.m., I walked back into my flat, looking forward to a nice, quiet evening at home. On my mind was leftovers from the lasagna I'd made Sunday evening and checking to see if I had any messages on the dating app. Slipping off my coat and shoes in my foyer in almost one fell swoop, I inhaled and then exhaled with relief, looked in the mirror, and smiled at the woman I saw before me. I'd had a great day at work today and was proud of who I was—if I never found a partner, I wanted to make sure those two facts remained.

Next, I went into motion in what had already become my routine after arriving home from work: I went to the bathroom, washed my hands, then walked into the living room to put some music on to have as my personal soundtrack as I heated up my food and settled in. It didn't take me long to decide which album was calling my name: Mariah's fun-loving and romantic-themed *Butterfly*. I grabbed the album from the bookshelf and placed it delicately onto my record player, making sure to connect the needle to the widest ring on the outermost edge of the vinyl record.

As "Honey" began to play, and Mariah's famous whisper tone mixed with the drums and piano notes from the Hitmen producers and Diddy's iconic ad-libs in the background, my legs automatically loosened up. Next thing I knew, I was dancing and singing my way to the kitchen. I pulled out my baking pan from the refrigerator and cut a huge slice of lasagna, plopping it onto a plate. While that warmed in the microwave, I grabbed some ingredients for a side salad. In one of the pearl-black bowls that came with the flat, I mixed baby spinach leaves, tomatoes, cucumbers, olives and a red wine vinaigrette dressing and then topped it with a sprinkle of Tony Chachere's Creole seasoning—a staple in my spice cabinet since befriending two New Orleanians in college.

Once both were ready, I danced my way back to the living room, where my small dining table sat in front of the floor-to-ceiling bay windows. The table was only large enough for two chairs, but it kept me from eating on my light gray couches at the glass coffee table in the same room—at least for now, because the couches were quite comfy. The last two things I needed were a glass of wine and my phone, both of which I retrieved while steadily dancing through my apartment, letting the album's change in tone as it moved to songs like "My All" and "The Roof" slow down my upbeat mood into something calmer for eating.

After a few amazing bites of my food, I decided it was time to take the plunge, opening my dating app to see if anyone I'd matched with had sent me a message. I was almost afraid to see that it might be empty, so I squinted just slightly and braced myself for the subtle but abundantly clear rejection of zero messages.

To my very pleasant surprise, there was one waiting for me, and it was from the guy I'd wanted to hear from the most… Jasper, a five-ten, blue-eyed Nicholas Hoult lookalike—at least when he was rocking a three-week-old beard.

Hi, Robin. It looks as if you either really like to read Nikki Giovanni or you thought a red book of poems might ward off any miscreants. Really hoping it's the former.

Okay, that was pretty cute, I thought, both rolling my eyes and smiling at the clever way Jasper let me know that he'd noticed the book in my photo—and that he, a white guy from the UK, knew who famed Black American poet Nikki Giovanni was.

I quickly typed a message back to him.

What if I admitted that it was a combination of both,

I asked, then picked up another forkful of my salad while I awaited his reply.

Both is also a satisfactory response, he messaged back in just a few minutes. Plus, it means you might be even more interesting than I assumed.

Okay, now I was intrigued, and far more invested in learning about Jasper than finishing my meal.

Do you have a lot of assumptions about me already, I questioned.

Not too many. Just the typical ones, such as you must like reading in parks, posing with red phone booths, taking candids in waterfalls and looking over your left shoulder at things.

I let out a huge laugh, appreciating the way Jasper used my profile photos to showcase his funny side.

Not bad guesses lol, I responded. And far better than my worst assumption about you, considering you have the same name as Kate Winslet's horrible ex-boyfriend in the movie The Holiday.

Oh no, don't tell me you're one of those Americans who watches stereotypical American movies about London life? Lol

Guilty as charged, Officer.

Well, I won't hold it against you for now, he replied. But only if you agree to a lunch date with me.

Deal. On one condition: it's a quick meetup. I learned the hard way recently that too long of a first date can turn into disaster.

Ha! Okay, I need to hear more about this, but don't worry, that works for me, too. You may decide to change your mind when we're in person, but in any case, your condition is met. Are you free on Friday?

Hmm, someone's confident, I replied. I'll have to tell my team to go to Nando's without me this week, but yes, I'm free.

Wonderful. Whereabouts do you work?

In The City. Just a block or so from St Paul's Cathedral.

Okay, then let's meet at Borough Market, he messaged back. Does that work for you?

I quickly looked at Google Maps on my phone to see how long it would take me to get there from my office—and, more importantly, how long it would take to get back if I needed to make a dramatic exit. Nine to fourteen minutes wasn't too bad.

Let's do it, I responded. I can't wait.

Part 2

"I don't know where I'm going from here, but I promise it won't be boring."

—David Bowie

Chapter Seven

That Friday afternoon, I apologized profusely to my team for ditching Nando's Fridays and, with my candy-red Telfar work bag in tow, made my way to Borough Market in hopes of meeting the man who'd been tickling my spirit through my cell phone the past couple days.

Unlike Daniel, Jasper didn't give off the vibes of a refined gentleman who delicately kissed women's hands when he met them. But that also meant he might not completely catch me off guard and end up one drink away from throwing up on me by the end of our date. What I really liked about him was that instead of charm, Jasper's strong point was his wit, as he cunningly kept me on my toes throughout our conversations. In the same way that I enjoyed being the person to have a sarcastic comeback when hanging with my friends, he seemed to relish getting the last word in ways that surprisingly made me smile when I talked to him. I was even starting to have some of those feels Rebecca suggested I look for.

Of course, Jasper was also super attractive, with his olive-toned skin and hair that made me dream about running my hands in it while cuddling with him. That didn't hurt, either.

We'd agreed to meet at Borough Market Kitchen, the food court addition to the eight-hundred-plus-year-old open-air market. There, Jasper had assured me, I'd find an outdoor but covered dining area that included some of the best food in all of London, even in the bitter cold. What he hadn't told me was the food court wasn't particularly easy to find, a fact that I soon learned as I wandered around for about ten minutes before finally getting my bearings and running into it on the north side of the market. I saw Jasper almost immediately, who surprisingly looked even better than he did on my phone.

As I walked up to him, my unbuttoned coat giving sneak peeks to my white–and–navy blue–striped long-sleeve shirt and dark mustard peplum pants, I was equally fascinated by the man and the rows of communal dining tables filled with people eating everything from overflowing pasta bowls to dumplings and meat skewers. Jasper, in a rust button-down peacoat and coffee-brown scarf, looked like he completely belonged among the people already gathered in the dining hall even as he stood near one of the food stands staring at his watch with a slightly annoyed look on his face.

"Well, hello there," I said, greeting him warmly and forgetting all formalities as I went in for a hug.

Thankfully, he didn't resist and squeezed me tightly, his arms wrapping around my body and holding me close, just long enough to remind me how good it felt to be in a man's arms. It was something I hadn't experienced since Eric and I broke up, and I hadn't realized how much I missed it until I found myself not wanting to let Jasper go. After a few more seconds, Jasper gently grabbed my forearms and guided me to be directly in front of him, just barely an arm's length away, so he could observe me in full view. His eyes traced down the length of my body with a sly smirk until he came back up to my face, biting his lower lip along the way.

Okay, maybe I was wrong about what drew me to him, I thought. Sure, I liked that he was funny, but my now-liquid legs were a telltale sign that he also had the ability to make me squirm in all the best ways.

"I'm glad you finally made it," he said, catching my eyes and not letting them go.

"Yeah, my friends call it RBJ time, sorry," I said, joking with him and batting my eyes to proclaim my innocence. "To be fair, this time it was because I had to find the spot, though. But aren't you happy I'm here now?"

"I am. I would have been happier if you were here two minutes ago."

His once-sly smirk turned into a clear frown of disappointment, and I wasn't sure how things had turned so quickly, especially over something as measly as a couple minutes.

"Seriously," I asked, hoping I could get Jasper back into the same jovial mood as I was. "You can't be that upset over two minutes, right? That's not even enough time to know for sure that someone's late. Like, maybe your watch is fast."

"My watch isn't fast," he said with a straight face.

"Okayyy, well, do you want me to leave?" I asked, now with my own annoyed tone. I had been really looking forward to this date, but suddenly I was concerned and silently wishing we could go back to the first moment when Jasper's hug seemed to envelop me and thoughts of blue-eyed brown babies ran through my head. And as much as I wanted to turn things around, I also wasn't going to be berated by someone right after meeting them for the first time.

Jasper took in a big, deep breath, closing his eyes and fixing his face all at once.

"No, it's fine," he replied with a sigh. "Clearly, I have a naughty girl on my hands who might have to be taught something different."

At that, the playful smirk I'd been hoping to see again returned, but not at all in the way I wanted, since I wasn't particularly keen on the idea of being *taught* anything—or better yet, spoken to like a child. It was becoming clear that maybe I'd gotten myself into yet another ridiculous dating situation that would be fodder for my friends. With a heavy sigh of my own, I tried once more to settle my annoyance and remind myself why we'd both wanted to see each other in the first place. Things had been so good over the phone the last two days as we talked about everything from our mutual love of American football to the ways that Sir Elton John's "Benny and the Jets" just hit you deep in your soul as soon it came on, so this was just a small hiccup, I told myself.

"Um, or not," I helpfully offered with a grin. "But can we maybe just start this greeting over, go back to you looking me up and down, and me being excited to see that crinkly smile of yours in person?"

"Oh, all right," he said, relenting. "But don't be so dodgy, Robin. I'm a cheeky chap. You can't take me too seriously, you know."

Jasper grabbed me back toward him so that our sides were almost stitched to each other in what felt like an attempt to right our ship, at least physically.

"Yes, that I do recall."

"And I wouldn't be me if I didn't give you a little hell for having me wait for you."

"You're right," I said thoughtfully. "That was unfair. My apologies."

"None needed. Let's go so I can show you the main event—hint, it's not me."

As Jasper took my hand in his, he smiled back at me warmly, like a kid who was suddenly over his temper tantrum. The only problem was I now noticed that while I'd offered up a mea culpa, he didn't seem to think it was necessary to apologize to *me* for his swift change in attitude. There was no way that was a good sign, but I steadied my breathing and tried to be positive. After all, I didn't need another text lecture from my friends about not giving men chances to make mistakes. Instead, I leaned into how good it felt having Jasper's fingers intertwined with mine and realized that he was holding my hand firmly, like someone who wasn't ready to let me go just yet. *Okay*, I thought, *maybe this is the guy I'd been talking to all this time.*

Following his lead, we started at the Mei Mei food stand, where Jasper ordered for us the poached chicken on rice with cucumber, coriander and chili-garlic sauce to go. Next, we went to La Tua Pasta, where he ordered a bowl of the spinach and ricotta ravioli for us to split. And finally he ordered some fish tacos from the Mexican food stand, Padre. With our gorgeous-looking and-smelling food in place, the two of us found an open section at one of the dining tables and began digging into our mishmash lunch.

"Now, *this* is the main event," he said, waiting for me to take my first bite of the poached chicken.

The Hainanese dish practically melted in my mouth as the flavors of the rice, chili-garlic sauce and chicken fused together on my tongue. He was right. This was totally worth the annoyance of not knowing where to go initially, dealing with his attitude and contemplating leaving all in a span of ten minutes, even if I wasn't exactly keen on him ordering for us. I just didn't want to ruin the good vibes we were finally starting to have, and to his credit, all the food looked, and so far, tasted fantastic.

"So good, yes?"

"Oh my God," I responded, unsure if I wanted to

savor my mouthful of food or chew it quickly to devour some more. "This is amazing!"

"So, you're saying I was right, then?" he asked, tilting his body toward me from across the table so he could clearly hear me say the words he'd already told me he was going to be waiting to hear.

"Yes, Jasper, you were right."

I smiled back at him, rolling my eyes playfully as I caught the smug look on his face from his accomplishment.

"That's all I needed to hear earlier, Robin, and we wouldn't even have had our little spat at the beginning," he said chuckling and then stuffing a taco in his mouth.

"I'll keep that in mind for the next time."

If there is a next time, I thought. As much as we were starting to get back to the rapport we'd had on the phone, I still wasn't entirely sure, and I felt like I was fighting against my instincts to leave him right at this dining table and head back to work. It was the nagging voice in my head repeating how I didn't give people chances that kept me seated where I was, however. And convinced to me at least try to do something different.

Sitting across from him, a wooden table in between us, in some ways felt the opposite of intimate. It didn't allow us to casually touch the other person's thigh or graze our fingertips while we talked or any of the other little ways people on dates showed their interest without words. It did, however, give me a clear view of Jasper's reactions to every word I spoke. And in that moment, I caught him crinkle his nose at my response. Then he forked some ravioli and leaned his body back slightly, plopping the pasta into his mouth and savoring every bite in a way that immediately showed on his face. When he finished, he looked back at me with a mischievous look in his eyes.

"Speaking of me being right, did you listen to the Leona Lewis song I mentioned the other night?" Jasper asked, reigniting a debate he'd started with me about which singer had the best voice.

From his perspective, it was Leona by a hair, arguing that Mariah's whistle-tone notes were nothing special, since the likes of Deniece Williams and Minnie Riperton had originally paved the way. I, of course, didn't agree and made the point that while Deniece and Minnie were pioneers, there was a reason Mariah had been succeeding in the business for more than thirty years. It wasn't just the whistle tone. It was her songwriting, her ability to produce, her five-octave range, the magic of her whisper vocals, the way she melded hip-hop beats with her beautiful tone—the whole nine. None of this had me inclined to change my opinion by listening to one Leona Lewis song, no matter how good.

"I did," I answered hesitantly. "But you're still not right on that front! I'm never going to say that she's a better singer than Mariah Carey."

I laughed, shaking my head at his foolish insistence but also glad that we were once again talking about something that we could at least get into a debate about. That's where we seemed to shine together, and maybe Jasper knew that, too. It was the only logical reason he was still trying to argue this point.

"Oh, come on. I know she doesn't have the catalog Mariah has, but we're just talking voice here."

Jasper's blue eyes twinkled from across the table. I could tell he was in his zone now, ready to be a reactionist and arrogantly engage me in a debate that was at once infuriating but would also make me consider taking off the rest of the day so that we could go back to my place and have sweaty, *I can do anything better than you*–type sex.

"Well, if we were talking catalog, there'd be no discussion," I said, twirling my fork into the air before poking it into the pasta dish to try the ravioli next. "I mean, honestly. There still isn't a discussion, but I'm trying not to get on my high horse and start listing all the number-one hits Mimi has had. Nineteen, you'll recall."

"But again, that's catalog. We're talking voice."

"I *am* talking voice," I responded quickly. "It's not just the number of hits. It's also the range of voice in them. How many singers do you know with singles reaching the high notes in 'Emotions' *annnnd* the low notes she hits in 'Sweetheart'? I can't name any! And certainly not Leona Lewis—who, don't get me wrong, has a great voice. But you just can't compare her to thee Mariah Carey."

"'Sweetheart' was a number-one song?" Jasper asked, still trying to win this debate on technicalities.

"No, but it was on her album *#1's* and was very popular in Black America," I shot back defiantly with an air of *I'm ready to play your little semantic games* in my voice.

Jasper stared back at me with a pleased smile on his face. He was definitely enjoying this as much as I was.

"Okay, so then who can be compared to Mariah Carey in your eyes?" he asked.

"No one." I lifted my eyes from the food to meet his and grinned widely. "She's incomparable."

"Sort of like you, her favorite fan?" he asked with a smirk.

"I'd like to think I'm pretty special, but whether or not I'm incomparable should probably be left up to other people to say."

I paused for a bit, tried a bite of the pasta and winked at my potential paramour across the table.

"What would you say?" I asked.

"You certainly seem to be one of a kind."

"In all the best ways, of course," I helpfully finished for him.

"Of course," he said, returning my wink and using his fork to scoop up some of the rice and poached chicken mixture, making sure to add a bit of the cucumber to it as well.

"How about me? Do you think I'm one of a kind?" he asked.

"Oh, Jasper, you are even more than that. You are funny, confounding, exceedingly handsome, arrogant in maybe the best ways and someone who pushes me to be incredibly clear about what I'm saying, because you are always at the ready to turn a word into a joke, a debate or a double entendre."

I sat back into my seat, giggling to myself and remembering how just the night before he'd caught me off guard responding to my comment that my day had been long and hard by remarking, "That's what she said." At the time, I'd busted out laughing, happy for the moment of levity after having crawled into bed at almost midnight.

But when I looked back over the table at Jasper, his face was beet red and a scowl had formed on his mouth.

"What's that about?" he asked.

"What do you mean?"

I was genuinely confused and once again trying to figure out how his mood had changed so quickly.

"I just told you that you're one of a kind, and you respond by crapping all over me?"

"What? No! How did I do that?"

"I'm confounding. Arrogant. Someone who twists your words all the time. Why would I want to be called those things?"

"Well, that's not how I meant it," I said, realizing suddenly how my words might have come off to him. But ironically, he *was* in fact twisting my words as he was fuming about being told that he did so. And I hadn't even intended my comment to be negative... at first.

"Whatever. You seem to be a very selfish individual, Robin."

Jasper spewed out his words with the quiet politeness of a British gentleman not wanting to cause a scene, but they did their damage all the same, puncturing the insecurities in my heart that I had managed to keep hidden for so long.

"Beautiful, but selfish. But maybe that's why you're

single at thirty. No one wants to marry a self-centered woman."

Wow. I was straight up looking at Mr. Hyde in the flesh and suddenly thankful I hadn't wasted more time on this man who really was the epitome of the Jasper in the movie *The Holiday.* Turns out, I'd called it from the beginning. Rude, condescending and so wishy-washy with his emotions, if I stayed around any longer, he was destined to take me on a roller coaster with him… and I refused.

Without another word, I stood up from the table, grabbed my work bag and stormed away from him. The clock on my cell phone told me that if I could get back to The City in less than twenty minutes, I might still be able to catch some of my team lingering at Nando's— where I should have been today in the first place—and remind myself of the joy I felt being in London. I was determined not to let some guy I'd just met on a dating app a few days ago ruin the rest of my day or how I felt about the whole of the UK.

I retraced my steps back to where I'd entered the market, walking past scores of people buying fresh produce and seafood, presumably for dinner with their families later in the evening. Meanwhile, I was fighting back angry tears and pissed that I'd allowed myself to go against my instincts and get berated by some guy who had the nerve to insult me for being thirty and single when he was ten years my senior and divorced.

Ugh, no convincing, Robin, I muttered under my breath. *You know better. This is what happens when you don't follow your gut.*

I was steps away from entering the London Bridge Underground station when I felt a familiar hand on my wrist. Instantly, I jerked it away and glared back into Jasper's eyes.

"I can't believe you just walked away like that," he said, staring daggers into me. "We were in the middle of a conversation."

"No, you were in the middle of a tirade," I responded calmly, not wanting to lose my cool and allow him to see just how furious I was—at him and at myself.

"You're simply not used to men being honest with you. I can tell."

That was it. I could no longer keep my cool. Every moment when I'd stood up for my friends raced through my head, and it didn't feel right that I wasn't doing the same when it came to my own life. I took in a deep breath and prepared to unleash holy hell on him.

"You are an insipid, insecure man," I said, stepping into his frame so that I could keep my voice down but ensure he would hear me. "I have no problems being told the truth. But you obviously like talking down to women, and that? I won't allow here."

I gestured to myself, pointing at my chest for emphasis.

"You want to talk truth? I came here today with an open mind and heart, excited to meet you. And from the moment I said hello, you've been nothing but antagonistic, chauvinistic, condescending and rude. I don't know if that normally gets you a second date, but let me be clear when I say that I am not at all interested in ever hearing from you or seeing you again. And you know what? It's my fault for sticking around as long as I did—I'll take that blame—but it stops here."

Jasper blinked his eyes in disbelief as I continued.

"Now, when I walked away from you at the table, I was trying to be kind. But you couldn't just leave it there and let it be, right? You had to come after me so you could try to have some kind of vicious last word, say something to make me doubt myself. Well, congratulations, you got your last word. And I got to have mine."

With that last sentence, I spun around on my nude pointed-toe flats with crisscross straps running from the toe to my ankle and entered the train station. As the train whooshed away from Borough Market, I thought about my friends and what they would have said if they were with me. Reagan would have been proud at how I left Jasper standing there with his mouth wide-open. Jennifer would have wanted to comfort me for being so hurt by his words. And Rebecca would have high-fived me for not completely blowing up on him and living up to whatever American stereotype he and others watching the scene take place had likely awaited. And yet I... I was just exhausted. There I was again, ending yet another date in disaster.

It had been funny when I was doing the dating pact in DC, regaling everyone with all my ridiculous stories. It was frustrating when it happened with the first guy in London. But now? Now, I was tired and sad about the fact that I was no closer to having the love I desired, even after giving up what felt like a sure thing with Eric because I believed in my heart something better was out there for me. With a second awful date under my belt, I was beginning to question if the problem was me. Jasper was right about one thing—I was thirty and all alone. I'd moved to a new city, heck, a new country, thinking that life would be different. Still, in just a few hours, I was going to be heading home, solo again, on a Friday night. And it wasn't as if I hadn't been trying. I'd been in therapy for years. I'd learned more about myself and my fears than I ever thought possible. I never stopped dating. I'd even tried giving someone multiple chances today when I knew it wasn't right in the first few minutes.

And what did I have to show for it?

Nothing was different.

Tears threatened to fall down my face, but one thing I was clear on was that I wasn't going to be the elegantly dressed Black woman crying on the Tube. And I certainly wasn't going to go back into my office, face puffy and eyes swollen, and stare down my team trying to decide if they should console me or pretend as if they didn't notice. Not today. I wiped my sweaty hands on my peacoat, swallowed down my feelings and put on the mask that had been serving me well for so long—the confident, capable, unflappable Robin Bridget Johnson.

By the time I walked back into my office, that would be who was there for everyone to see.

Chapter Eight

"Cheers to the weekend," I screamed over the music blaring through the speakers not ten feet away from us.

I raised my glass high into the air, prompting the three immaculately dressed and red-lipped women partying with me to do the same.

"We'll drink to that!" shouted Olivia and her friends Nneka and Tracy, invoking the now-infamous call-and-response chant derived from Rihanna's classic ode to Jameson and drinking shots with your girls.

With a loud clank, we each tilted our heads back and poured the one and a half ounces of liquor down our throats, wincing as it warmed our chests and loosened our limbs that were totally ready for a night of singing and dancing.

Well, I couldn't speak for everyone else, but I knew I

was ready. A week after another disastrous date, I was thrilled to say that my Friday could not have looked more different if I'd wished on a star and had all my dreams come true. On this night, at a nightclub in Shoreditch, I found myself flanked by some of the most beautiful women I'd ever met, and somehow—thankfully for me—I was managing to blend in just fine with them. Liv looked stunning as her Fenty 460 skin tone glowed under the warm lights of the club, matched only by the long-sleeved auburn satin minidress with cutouts that showcased her slim torso. Nneka, with her envious and all-natural hip-to-waist ratio, stood next to me wearing a deceivingly low-cut black bandage dress that looked as if it had been painted on her. Tracy, who was somehow blessed with perfect D-cup breasts, a butt that J. Lo would worship and dimples in both her cheeks, rocked a leopard-print slip dress that dropped to right below her knees. And I had chosen a dark gold silk skirt that fell to midcalf on my left side with a wide slit that rose to right above my thigh on my right side. Paired with that, I wore a black lace tank top, a black blazer and silver ankle-strap heels.

We were incredibly overdressed, but on purpose. On a night when we all needed to step out and feel good about ourselves for various reasons, we hadn't wanted to do so in jeans and blouses. After drinking our shots at the bar, we grabbed our regular glasses of liquor and headed to the main section of the nightclub to get our spots before the main attraction—Cleo Sol—came on the stage. Each one of us had different reasons for loving her music. Nneka could relate to her songs about motherhood, Tracy loved the velvety tone Cleo used to express her personal experiences, I longed for the joy you could literally feel in some of her songs about love and Liv felt like Cleo's jazzy intermix of neo soul and funk music spoke to her soul.

"Cheers also to you fabulous girls," Olivia shouted out, raising her second glass in the air after we'd found the perfect spot to the left of the stage, where we could see everything unimpeded and still feel like we were part of the crowd.

"Cheers!" we all shouted in unison as the lights dimmed around us and the band began playing the soft syncopations at the beginning of "Rose in the Dark," the song that was also the name of her latest album.

For the next twenty minutes, we sang along with Cleo Sol as if we were her backup singers, completely in our own world, forgetting the other people in the crowd—who likely also felt as if they were in their own private concert. It wasn't until I heard the beautiful tenor voice behind me singing along to "When I'm in Your Arms" that I remembered we were not in fact alone.

I turned my head around to see the face matching the voice, and my knees almost buckled under me. He was gorgeous, with thick eyebrows, short jet-black hair, just enough of a beard to sculpt his face and eyes that looked like the kindest soul was behind them.

He smiled back at me as I tried to stop staring, his lips curling up slightly to reveal the pearl-white teeth underneath them, somehow also controlling my mouth, which formed into a smile as well. My eyes traced the length of him until, like a puppet, I was pulled back up to his pupils, caught in a trance that wouldn't let either of us go. As the song transitioned to "Sideways" and Cleo Sol and this beautiful stranger sang to me about finding love, I was sure I'd been pulled into some sort of time warp, where everything except he and the music were wiped away.

Hi, he mouthed to me, totally catching me staring at him.

"Hi."

"I'm Zayn."

"Robin."

"Pleasure to meet you, Robin."

Zayn moved his body closer to me so that suddenly there was barely air between our limbs. I turned my head back around to face the stage but could feel the soft tickles of his clothes touching my skin and his lips hovering just above the top of my head even with me standing five-nine with three-inch heels on.

"You are...entrancing," he whispered into my ear and gently took hold of my right hand, still at both of our sides.

I closed my eyes and decided to give in to the moment, letting Zayn's buttery voice soothe me back into our time warp world, where nothing else mattered.

By midnight, the lights were back on, the crowd of people was beginning to disperse and Zayn and I were attempting to participate in the hilarious group conversation around us that was jumping from the last time each person had fallen down some steps to tips on how to make sure baby boys don't urinate on you when changing their diapers. The only problem was that Zayn and I seemed to be having a hard time unlocking from each other's eyes and thus contributing anything meaningful at all to the discussions.

"Wow, so you're a background singer?" Liv asked Zayn, recalling to one of the first things he'd mentioned to our group when he and his friends formally introduced themselves twenty minutes before.

"Yeah, I am," he responded, finally unleashing himself from my eyesight.

"That's really cool."

"It has its ups and downs, yeah, but I love it."

"Sure, that's understandable," she said.

"Yo, tell them about the time you thought you were going to be singing with Floetry after they reunited only for them to break up again," Zayn's friend Hassan said, playfully slapping him on the arm while cracking up laughing.

"Nah, bruv, I think we'll save that for another day," he responded sheepishly and returned to his search for my eyes again.

Quickly capturing them, we stood in front of each other for a quiet few seconds, blocking out everyone once again before bringing our attention back to the conversation at hand.

"And what are you three gentlemen getting into tonight?" I asked, attempting to actually, finally, join in.

"From here, not much," said Hassan. "The wife and kids only gave me permission to be out but for so long tonight."

"Yeah, and I'm not married, but I don't think my girlfriend would be too happy with me coming home after one," said his other friend, Syed. "Our boy Zayn here, though, is completely single and good to hang out longer, yeah, Zayn?"

Syed elbowed Zayn in his side to get his attention, which had seemingly wandered back my way.

"Yeah, yeah, I'm free," he said, clearing his throat. "I don't have plans or anyone waiting at home for me."

A smile I couldn't control grew on my face at the thought of getting to spend more time with him—and confirmation that he was indeed single.

"Well, that's good," I said. "Maybe you can join us for a nightcap or a small meal before we all head home?"

"Actually, babe, I need to go home, too," Liv interrupted as she scrunched up her face in an apology. "You know my pumpkin fades after midnight. It's already past my bedtime now."

"Yeah, me, too," added Nneka, shrugging her shoulders. "The hubby and kids, you know."

"Me, too, babe," Tracy said.

"Right, right, of course," I said, my voice clamming up at the thought of everyone going home and losing my chance to spend a few more hours in Zayn's presence. "Well, that just leaves me and you?"

I looked back at Zayn, hoping he wouldn't say no, too.

"That works for me," he said softly, taking my right hand in his again and gently pulling me to his side. "Is that good with you?" he asked, whispering directly into my ear.

"Uh-huh." My eyes fluttered closed as a small shiver went down my spine.

"Okay, then."

Zayn turned back to look at everyone else, who were each standing staring at us gobsmacked by the steamy chemistry in front of them.

"Yeah, somehow I don't think we'll be missed," Liv muttered aloud, causing the whole group to break out into laughter.

"Okay, okay, get your laughs in now," I said back to them.

"Oh, we will, babe. Don't worry," she responded, high-fiving Hassan. "But we also want you both to have a good time tonight."

She winked at me as a text came through my phone.

And don't overthink it, the text read. Have fun with Zayn. You deserve to feel as pretty as he obviously thinks you are.

I replied back with a simple smiley face emoji and looked back at my friend with the same emotion on my face. We'd known each other for about a month, but she was quickly becoming a good friend—one who knew when I just needed the reminder to keep myself in the moment and enjoy what was right in front of me.

"You ready?" asked Zayn, jolting me out of my thoughts.

"Oh, yes, absolutely."

"Great, because I know just the spot where we can go."

"As long as it's not in Islington or Borough Market, I'm down," I said, chuckling to myself. I had no desire to revisit my last disastrous encounters.

"That's wildly specific, but no," he responded. "I was thinking pizza right up the street."

"Oh my God, that's perfect," I said, throwing my head back in mock ecstasy.

Zayn raised his left eyebrow and looked deep into my eyes with a smirk that had the power to make me feel like he was undressing me in front of everyone.

"Duly noted," he said, clearing his throat once again and starting to walk us to the door.

"Let me know when you make it home safely," I asked, turning back to lock eyes with Liv, Nneka and Tracy. It was a habit I'd picked up with my friends back in the States, where we always made sure we arrived safely to our next destination after spending time with each other, whether it was broad daylight or 2:00 a.m.

"All right, and have fun, you two," Liv shouted from behind us.

"We will," we replied in unison.

"And don't anything we wouldn't do," added Hassan.

"We will!"

Zayn and I burst out laughing and walked outside into the cold winter air. It was the perfect excuse for him to wrap his muscular arms around me as we made our way to the next spot, and I didn't mind it one bit.

Chapter Nine

Two weeks, three dates and countless texts later, I found myself still enamored with the background singer whose eyes seemed to have a magical hold on me. This fact was made even clearer every time I tried to knock my golf ball into a hole but made the catastrophic mistake of looking at him first, getting lost in his smile and completely missing the ball. Which I'd just done three times in a row.

"You're doing this on purpose!" I screamed out as my minigolf putter swung into the air once again.

Zayn's deep laugh was like surround sound in our part of the course.

"It's not my fault you keep getting distracted."

"It actually, quite literally, is," I corrected him.

"Would you prefer it if I stood behind you, then, while you're taking your shot?"

"No, because then I'm going to be thinking about how good it would feel to have you wrap me in your arms from behind."

"Mmm, that's not a bad idea, yeah."

Zayn walked closer to me, his eyes still staring intensely into mine.

"And then maybe I could even help you finally hit the ball," he said, pulling me into his arms and swinging me around.

After one full twirl, he planted my feet back firmly on the bright green Astroturf, kissed me on my forehead and swiped the left side of my butt cheek with his hand before getting into position to take his turn. It all happened so fast, I barely realized what he was doing until I saw him swing his putter and land the ball right in the middle of the hole.

"You've got to be kidding me," I muttered under my breath.

"All's fair in love and war, babes."

Zayn came toward me again and kissed me on the left side of my face, right in the crease between my lips and my cheek. It was fast and soft, just like the forehead kiss, a symbol of comfort and ease among us— and not at all intended to be sexual, except each time it still happened to send quivers down my spine. In fact, any time Zayn looked at me—touched me, spoke my name in his mixed British and Pakistani accent, really and truly did anything in my direction—I felt like I was going to melt into his arms.

It was bad, especially since my desire for him was affecting my performance during crazy golf, but it also felt really nice to be this into someone again. I hadn't had this kind of a sustained attraction to anyone since Eric, and unlike the prince, Zayn and I had been spending nearly all our time learning about each other while exploring different parts of London together.

Tonight was crazy golf on Oxford Street. The date before, we had drinks on a rooftop overlooking the city, and before that we'd found ourselves singing our hearts out at a karaoke bar in Soho. And somehow, each night, despite the way my insides tingled and craved his touch, I managed to let Zayn take me home, kiss me goodbye and leave without giving in to the voice screaming in my head and wanting me to say to him, "Come upstairs and take me now, please." This was all because I'd made the critical decision the night that we met that I wanted to take things slowly so I could give my brain a chance to see if he was the guy for me before I let my heart and vagina weigh in. My resolve was clearly dissipating with each tender peck from Zayn's lips, however, so I did the only thing I had left in my arsenal—pouted and fake stomped away.

"Aw, don't be like that, babes. You'll get another turn," Zayn teased me, poking me in my side.

"You know I'm an only child, and I don't like to lose."

"And I'm an oldest, yeah, so I can't just let you win. Plus, it's more fun watching you squirm and not try to jump my bones, anyway."

"Oh my God!"

"Just saying," he replied, shrugging his shoulders and walking us to the next part of the course. "Come on, it's your turn again."

"Okay, but this time, try not to be so seductive, please?" I begged as I got into position again to try to hit my ball.

"Can I ask questions? Maybe that will make me less enticing to you," he said, laughing and raising one of his thick eyebrows.

"Yes, sure, let's try some questions."

"All right, do you think you're so close with your friends because you're an only child?"

Zayn stood just to my right side, slightly out of my periphery. And with my concentration fully on the ball this time, I leaned into my putter, lightly swung back and finally, finally struck it.

"Yes!" I screamed out, jumping up and down as if I'd hit a hole in one. In reality, I was still probably at least two more swings from getting the ball in the hole, but I'd made contact, at least. That was better than I could say before.

I turned back to look at Zayn, whose face was shining brightly at me.

"Congratulations," he said. "Maybe the trick really is for me to be out of your eyesight."

He walked toward me again, making sure to casually slide his hand across my torso as he passed me to get into position for his turn. I chose not to comment on the touch, though I felt the familiar tingle in my spine as his fingertips grazed the skin between my crop top and acid-washed mom jeans.

"Maybe so," I replied, straightening my back. "Okay, but back to your question."

I thought about my response for a second as I watched Zayn line up his putter with the ball, and just as he swung, I answered.

"I think that might be true," I said. "I know it's a big part of the reason I wanted to go to a historically Black university. I was looking for community, having not really grown up in a big family. I mean, I'm an only child, but also, I don't have a lot of cousins, either— so even my friends in high school were really important to me. And then when I got to Howard, I lucked up and met the most amazing women my first week at school and sort of haven't looked back."

Even as I spoke, I stared in horror as Zayn's ball rolled to within less than an inch of the hole. When it finally stopped, he looked back up at me with his signature full-face smile and shrugged again.

"Cute try," he said. "But you see, while I too want nothing more than to take your lips with mine and suck on them until you're whispering my name and begging me for more, my desire to beat you at this game won't let you distract me."

Ugh, there went that shiver again.

"What? I was just answering the question *you* asked me," I responded, feigning innocence with fluttery eyes.

"Sure, and it just happened to be right as I swung."

"Oh, is that what happened?" I asked, biting my lower lip.

"It is," he said, walking up to me again and stopping

in front of me just so there were barely a few centimeters in between us. Slowly, he leaned into my neck and whispered his next words to me. "And you didn't succeed, so maybe you have to try harder next time."

"What do you think that should look like?" I asked him in the same whisper, struggling not to grab his back and dig my hands into him, or even just close my eyes as I took in his scent.

"Mmm, I have a lot of ideas, dear Robin, but probably none of them are appropriate for crazy golf." Zayn took his right hand and slowly dragged it down my back, the nails of his fingers barely touching me but causing me to arch into him so that our chests pressed against each other and my neck opened up for him. "So, maybe we just continue talking about our friends and family, yeah?"

He leaned away from me and motioned his arm to the side to show it was my turn again. And I took in a deep breath before attempting to walk, thankful I was wearing my crisp white Chuck Taylors and not a pair of heels, because I would have surely lost my balance with my knees buckling like they did around him.

Clearing my throat, I responded, "Yeah," and took my turn again.

"So, do you miss them? Your friends," asked Zayn as I got into swinging position.

"All the time. But I was also ready for something new, something that was all me, you know?"

"I hear you. I have that feeling sometimes being from such a big family, and then being the oldest, too. It's a lot of pressure on me to set an example all the time, be the model. I've thought about moving to America, actually, to chart my own path, not have to worry about whether I'm living up to my parents' expectations or not."

"Well, I can tell you from experience, leaving the country doesn't stop you from worrying about that. I managed to earn this huge promotion that brought me to London, and I still feel like I'm a disappointment sometimes to my parents because all they really want is for me to find a husband."

"Well, there's one thing we have in common—parents waiting for us to get hitched and make them some grandchildren."

"That's true," I said, laughing. "And this."

I leaned into my putter once more, swung and hit the ball straight into the hole.

"Hell yes!" I shouted out, jumping around once again.

I was midtwirl when I felt Zayn's hands around my waist, gently pulling my body into his as he placed his lips on top of mine. Time stood still as our lips intertwined, tongues darting in and out of our mouths and our breaths growing heavy between us. My hands instinctively went to the nape of his neck, grabbing strands of hair along the way, while his hands traveled to the small of my back, fingering light circles where my belt touched the open air underneath my top.

Finally, after a couple minutes, we pulled away from each other, both of us seemingly remembering where we are at the same time.

"Ahem, sorry," Zayn said, staring into my eyes. "Winning just looks really good on you."

I raked my hands through my hair, letting some of the blond tendrils fall into my face.

"I've been trying to tell you this all night," I responded with a wink.

"Now I get what you mean."

By midnight, Zayn and I were walking, hand in hand, back to my apartment, our bodies almost plastered to each other as my head rested slightly on his shoulder and his other arm draped over mine.

"If you want, you can spend the night tonight," I said, lifting my head to gaze into his gorgeous eyes.

"Oh really?" he asked with another eyebrow raise.

"Mmm-hmm."

I was done holding back with him, and my brain, heart and vagina were in all agreement that it was time to see if our chemistry was as palpable when we lost our clothes as it was just anticipating it.

"I think I might like to take you up on that."

Zayn bent his head down toward my face and planted another soft kiss on my lips, sliding his tongue in and out and lingering just long enough to leave me breathless.

"Ooh, Z, I'm telling!"

Neither of us saw who belonged to the voice that appeared from our left side, but by Zayn's reaction, and her use of a nickname, he clearly immediately knew who it was. With whiplash speed, Zayn straightened up and moved slightly aside from me, thankfully still holding on to my hand, at least.

"Alaya," he said without even looking her way at first. Instead, he fixed his eyes on me as if to convey his apologies ahead of time. *My sister*, he mouthed.

"Fancy meeting you out here, brother," she said, grabbing ahold of his shoulders and shaking them. "And who's this? C'mon! Introduce us, why don't ya?"

"Alaya, this is Robin," Zayn said, gesturing between the two of us. "Robin, this is my sister Alaya."

"Nice to meet you," I replied, dropping Zayn's hand so that I could lift mine to shake hers.

"Oh, American!"

Alaya shook my hand with a big smile, but she also took a moment to not-so-subtly drag her eyes from my hair down to my shoes. It was pretty obvious that I was being sized up in the way only a sister can—with a huge smile so that her brother didn't know the difference but the woman was perfectly clear it was happening.

"Sorry," she said finally after finishing her appraisal.

I hoped that her apology was to the fact that she realized she'd blurted out my nationality instead of also saying it was nice to meet me.

"The accent gives you lot away," she continued, shrugging.

"It's quite all right. I'm used to it at this point," I offered meekly, noting silently that her apology had not been for the reason I wanted.

Thankfully, Alaya soon turned her attention back to

her brother, playfully poking him in his side. Clearly, I realized, their entire family was very hands-on.

"So, what are you two lovers getting into?" she asked. "Well, you know, other than smooching on the public streets."

"Ahem, we're actually just leaving crazy golf," Zayn responded, grabbing my hand in his again and pulling me to him as his long arms wrapped around me. "What are you doing? You're not out here by yourself, are you?"

"Of course not, bruv," she answered, pointing her arm out to the group of five standing off to the side. "My friends and I were just leaving a gathering when I saw my brother suffocating this poor woman with his tongue down her throat, so I had to come see what the fuss was about."

"I can assure you—"

Zayn tried to respond, but Alaya promptly interrupted him.

"No, no. Never you mind. I'm just being a bit cheeky with you, yeah? Really, I just wanted to come say hi, and just my luck, I got to meet the lovely Robin."

She raised her eyebrow at me, using the same motion that Zayn always did, but for some reason, hers felt more accusatory than playful. I tried to get out of my head and continue playing along, deciding that it was better to allow Zayn's sister to poke fun at us than to risk upsetting someone so close to the man I was starting to really enjoy spending lots of time with.

"I'm the lucky one," I responded, making sure to keep my teeth showing brightly. "Zayn talks about his family a lot, but I didn't think I'd get to meet anyone this soon."

"Well, don't believe everything he says, yeah. We don't torture him nearly as much as he lets on."

"It's been nothing but good things, I promise."

"You shouldn't believe that, either," she said, letting out a loud laugh. "We're a bunch of scoundrels!"

"This is true," said Zayn, kissing the back of my neck.

The way his lips landed softly and quickly at my nape, just for a second or two, I could tell this was his way of letting me know he was there for me as his sister did her best silent detective work. It managed to both soothe me and bring back that spine-tingling feeling, just knowing that he cared enough to make such a subtle but significant gesture.

"And we should probably go so you can stop torturing Robin, too."

"Oh, me?" Alaya stepped back and looked around, feigning innocence. "You don't think I'm torturing you, right, Robin?"

"Of course, not," I said, smiling back at the woman who looked so much like my background-singer bae but who was clearly still trying to determine if she liked me or not. "Zayn is just being protective, I'm sure, right?"

I looked back and up at him, catching Zayn's eyes and trying to send telepathic messages to tell him that I was okay—but also that I really wanted to tear his clothes off as soon as we got back to my place. He must have understood my silent signal, because he almost immediately dipped his head down and kissed me again. This time, his kiss had an urgency behind it as his lips pressed into mine, causing my upper body to instinctively move into his to be as close as I could to him.

"Ahem, well, all right, I guess that's my cue," Alaya said from the side.

Her tone didn't sound annoyed, but it didn't sound happy, either. Maybe it was amused? Or intrigued? I wasn't sure. In fact, as much as I was trying, I simply couldn't pick up a clear vibe from her other than the obvious—that she was just as protective of her brother as he seemed to be of me. And that fact was starting to leave just the slightest unease in my throat.

"I'm sorry," I said turning back to her sheepishly. "Your brother—"

"Please. Say no more. I beg," she said, interrupting me.

"That's fair. It really has been nice to meet you, though."

"Maybe we could plan for something together next time, yeah?" Zayn asked, looking to us both.

"I'd really like that," I replied, staring back at him with the biggest grin and trying to hold in the happy squeal wanting to pour out of me, because two weeks in, the guy I was dating was talking about planning a double date with his sister. And better yet, the idea of that wasn't completely freaking me out and making me have thoughts of running away as fast as I could.

"Sure, that could be fun," said Alaya in a tone that

didn't really match her words. "You two run along, though. I have to get back to my peeps."

"Be safe, Ly," Zayn said, leaning toward her and kissing her on the cheek.

"Always do, Z. But do me a favor and check your phone in a bit, yeah?"

Alaya quickly returned Zayn's kiss on his cheek and skipped off to her friends before stopping once more to say a final word.

"Oh, and Robin!" she screamed back. "It was really nice to meet you, too, babes."

In that moment, with that small gesture from her, my smile couldn't have been brighter if a rainbow were next to me.

"Guess my sis liked you, huh?" Zayn asked as the group disappeared around the corner and we began walking again. "That's a win for me."

"Maybe. Are you sure, though? She seemed pretty iffy on me up until the very end."

"Yeah, you don't know my sister. That was her on her best behavior."

"Oh, I thought her behavior was just fine. I just couldn't tell if she liked me or wanted to kick me at first."

"It might have been a bit of both!"

"No thanks to you, who couldn't seem to keep his hands off me," I said, jokingly pushing him away. "I may not have my own sisters, but I know that they don't necessarily love watching their brother all over someone they just met."

Zayn grabbed me hands right as they landed on his

chest and pulled me back into him, leaning in close to my ear.

"I don't mind anyone knowing how much I like you, Robin. Plus, are you saying you don't like when my hands are on you?"

"That's not what I'm saying at all," I replied.

My face brimmed with pleasure, not just from being in such close contact with Zayn, but also because he'd just admitted to really liking me. That might not have normally been as big of a deal three dates in, but the way my dating luck had been lately, it was a welcome change. Not to mention, as hard as I had been trying to keep my cool, the feeling was starting to be pretty mutual.

"Just checking because I'm not sure if you know this, but your lips, when I kissed them, they were saying to me, 'Zayn, please take me. Now.'"

In a falsetto, Zayn slowly whispered the last part of his sentence in my ear, even attempting to put on an American accent.

"Is *that* what they were saying?" I asked, moving so that I placed my lips right above his, wanting to see if mine were the only ones that would beg for mercy.

Instead of looking at Zayn in his eyes, I stared deeply at the tiny space where our mouths almost but didn't quite touch. My breathing quickened as I lingered in his space, letting him feel my presence but not me.

"Mmm-hmm," he replied, seemingly unable to speak actual words any longer.

"And what were yours saying?" I asked.

"Yes, Robin. Anytime. Anyplace. Anywhere. Anyhow…you want it."

The two of us continued to play chicken with the other, waiting to see who would crack and move into the kiss first. I was determined not to let him win, but after replaying Zayn's last words over in my head, I let out a combination of a sigh and a moan into his mouth, needing to release at least something from my body. In a flash, he gave up, pressing his lips into mine and enveloping me into his embrace tightly.

"I think maybe I'm not the only one who wants the other right now," I said, giggling my way out of his arms even as I craved more of him all over me.

"That much is clear, babes. You and me, we're like Mariah and Derek Jeter—the chemistry we have could make albums worth of hot music."

My smile grew wide again as I finally let down my guard and snuggled into Zayn's chest while we continued walking. This was why I believed so strongly in my no-convincing rule, I thought. It had led me to a guy who was passionate about me, funny, unafraid to share his feelings—and not in a creepy or mood-swinging way—and he even fully understood how much a Mariah reference meant to me, even if it was a fairly dated one.

Floating on cloud nine, I walked hand in hand with Zayn the rest of the way to my apartment, our bodies practically glued together the entire time except when he momentarily pulled his phone out of his pocket to read a text. As quickly as that happened, however, he was right back in my bubble, intertwining his fingers with mine.

I did notice that his grip was slightly looser than before, however. But I tried not to overthink it, or the fact that Mariah and Derek Jeter didn't actually last very long.

Twenty minutes later, after walking nearly forty minutes hand in hand plus engaging in an impromptu visit with his sister, Zayn and I finally walked into my apartment building—the sea foam–green walls and tan flooring of the lobby reminding me that I was home and could finally rest my tired feet. Like the nights before, Zayn rode the elevator with me, walked me to my flat door and watched like a gentleman as I pulled out my keys and opened my door. This time, however, I was excited that he was going to be joining me when I crossed my threshold.

That was, until I noticed that his gray-loafered feet were still planted in the hallway as I began to walk inside.

"You're still coming in, right?" I asked jokingly. "I take my shoes off when I get in, not outside the door."

"Actually, um…"

I looked up at Zayn's face, probably for the first time in about fifteen minutes, since we'd been walking so close to each other, and suddenly I noticed something was different than before. The pure desire he'd shown when staring into my eyes had been replaced with a sadness that was confusing and concerning, and the alarm bells began ringing in my head.

"I think…it might be best…if I say good-night, actually, and talk to you tomorrow."

Zayn's voice was hesitant but firm, and I knew instantly he'd made up his mind long before he stopped short of walking into my foyer. Even the way his body all of a sudden seemed to lean away from me sort of reminded me of my demeanor when breaking up with Eric. The difference, though, was that I hadn't been tonguing Eric down just moments before I ended our relationship.

With a deep breath, I calmed down my thoughts and attempted not to jump to the worst conclusion—something that was so easy to do when you've been blindsided as much as I had in the past. Zayn hadn't said he was ending anything, I said to myself. In fact, he hadn't said much else other than that he would talk to me tomorrow. So I needed to simply take him at his word and not move us two steps ahead into my worst fear. Not when we'd had such a good night—one that even included him saying to his sister that he wanted us to go on a double date.

"Okay," I replied. "Can I ask—"

"I just think it's best tonight," Zayn answered before I could finish my question.

It was clear I wasn't going to get anything else out of him, so I figured it was better to end things and look forward to talking in the morning.

"Okay, then," I said. "I understand."

I walked back out of my foyer to give Zayn a hug, since he still hadn't moved an inch, as if he was afraid that he'd get caught in quicksand if he stepped any closer to my door. Wrapping his arms around me, he held me tightly and softly kissed my forehead as he said a quiet "good night." Then, before I could say anything in return, he pivoted and walked back to the elevator.

I didn't know it then, but the brief moment I spent watching Zayn walk down my hallway, turn and wave goodbye once more would end up being the last time I ever saw him in person.

Chapter Ten

The next morning, I woke up to the sound of my cell phone ringing bright and early at 9:00 a.m. on a Saturday. I'd had a hard time sleeping the night before, wondering what had changed in the fifteen to twenty minutes between Zayn telling me he wanted me anyhow, anywhere, anytime to him limping out of my apartment building, his head hanging low. This meant that I was especially groggy and slow to answer my phone, but as I came out of my slumber, dread quickly washed over me.

No one really calls anymore, I thought, wiping the sleep out of my eyes. At least not before they texted and asked if you were free for a call. About the only people who still did were my parents, and even they had learned to text unless it was really important. In the past, Reagan or Jennifer might call if Christine had an emergency. But, well, that reason was no longer valid. Either way, all I knew was that a call on a Saturday morning, especially when it was 3:00 and 4:00 a.m. in Chicago and DC respectively, meant only one thing—something was wrong.

I leaned over the side of my bed and pulled my phone off the nightstand, answering it without even bothering to look at whose name was on the screen.

"Robin?" a familiar voice asked.

"Yeah," I answered, still half-asleep.

"Hey, it's Zayn."

Crap.

I immediately shot up in bed, my heart dropping into the mattress.

"Hey, Zayn, is everything all right?"

"Actually—" He hesitated, sounding eerily similar to the way his voice did when he stopped himself from entering my apartment. "I know it's early, but I figured I should call you and let you know what happened last night."

"Oh? Okay, it must be really important to call at 9:00 a.m., but honestly, I was wondering, so I appreciate the call."

"You're right, it's early. I'm sorry."

"No, no, it's fine, really. Talk to me."

Zayn paused for a moment, maybe gathering himself on the other end of the phone. In the silence, I waited with bated breath for him to say more.

"Well, I want to start by apologizing for being so

weird at the end of the night. I had a lot on my mind, and I didn't really know what to do, so I—"

"It's okay," I interrupted, hoping that it came off as reassuring—to us both. "Look, if you weren't comfortable spending the night last night, like, that's fine. I get it. I know it's one thing to joke about taking the next step and something else entirely to do it."

"It's not that," Zayn replied. "The truth is, I got a text last night while we were walking to your flat. It was a family friend telling me that she was back in London."

He paused again, and I sat completely still in my bed, as if moving would somehow make what I felt in my bones he was getting ready to say come faster. The events of the night flashed in front of me. Of course, I remembered the text and how he'd seemed to distance himself ever so slightly after he read it. Other women might not have even noticed it, but I did. Experience had long taught me to be on guard for small changes in a man's body language, even or maybe especially when I liked him.

"Okay," I said, attempting to break the silence. It was one thing to try to delay the inevitable, but now my chest was tight with negative anticipation, so I needed him to just say it.

"And well, I guess she wanted to let me know that she loved me and wanted us to be together."

"Whoa, what?" I shouted out. "Wait, can we back up? This family friend just randomly texted you that she loved you?!"

As much as I was preparing myself for the worst,

even I hadn't expected *those* words to come out of Zayn's mouth. Was he telling me that some random lady just texted him out the blue expressing her love for him? Seriously? In what world…?

"I know. It probably seems very unbelievable."

"I mean, right now, anything is on the table, I guess," I said, shaking my head at the ridiculousness I'd gotten myself into this time. I took in another deep breath before broaching the only question I needed an answer to after that kind of revelation.

"So, okay, Zayn. I guess the million-dollar question is do you love her, too?"

The silence on the other end of the phone told me everything I needed to know, and tears began to slowly pour down my face. Once again, I was going to be the one left all by herself, and this time it wasn't because I'd convinced myself to settle for less—it was because I just hadn't been good enough. I could see my tombstone in my head: Robin Bridget Johnson—successful businesswoman, ride-or-die friend, amateur fashionista who never found love.

I wiped away my tears and waited for Zayn to speak. I wasn't going to let him get away without at least being honest with me, especially since he hadn't even had the decency to do it in person.

"Yes," he finally said quietly.

"Oh? You do."

I fought back my tears again, not wanting to give him the pleasure of hearing me cry, swallowing down all the memories of us flirting and getting to know each other over the past couple weeks.

"Yeah, Robin, I'm terribly sorry. I—"

"No, no, it's… I…"

For once, I was at a loss for words. Here I'd been once again falling for someone unavailable, who apparently secretly loved someone else, and just my luck—she decided to tell him right as we were getting close.

"What did she say, exactly, Zayn?" I asked, suddenly needing to know more, as if finding out the nitty-gritty details would stave off the pain that I felt swelling in my chest.

"In the text?"

"Yeah, I… I need to know what she said."

"Just that, well, I guess Alaya mentioned to her that she saw us. And that I seemed to really like you. So, if she was going to say something to me, then she better say it now. And that's when she did. She texted, 'The thing is Z, I love you.'"

Wow, the damn sister, I thought, falling back into the cushions of my bed. I knew it. I flipping knew it. He'd tried to make me second-guess myself, but every fiber in my body told me that she had been up to something, and this clearly confirmed I was right.

"And you read all that last night while with me, in your arms, walking to my flat, with me fully under the impression that we were going to make love? Right?"

It wasn't like I didn't know the answers at this point, but I was having a hard time wrapping my head around it all, so the likely-rhetorical questions came pouring out of my mouth before I could stop them.

"Well, that's why I couldn't come in last night," he responded. "Truthfully, I didn't know what to do. I just knew it wouldn't be right to have sex with you when I wasn't sure how I felt about her message."

"And how do you feel this morning?" I asked, closing my eyes and bracing for the worst.

"Like, I really like you," he said. "My sister was right. She could see how into you I am."

Zayn paused again before continuing.

"But also, Robin, I've loved Samaya since I was a teenage boy. And I just think I have to take this chance with her. If I don't, I—"

"No, I get it," I said, unable take any more of what had turned out to be a very prolonged rejection. It was the end; we just needed to go ahead and say it.

"So, this it, then."

It wasn't a question this time. I had no more questions left in me.

"I'm really sorry, Robin."

"No, it's fine," I said back defiantly. "Tell your sister I said thanks, though."

"For what?"

"For reminding me that I'm not the girl who gets to be happy in love. I needed that."

"Robin—"

"Please, Zayn. Enough. Thank you for calling, and you know what? I truly do wish you and Samaya well."

I hung up the phone before I could hear him say another word and quickly pulled the covers over my head. If I could have blocked out the world in that moment, I would have. As it was, blocking out the sunlight from my window would have to do.

* * *

The next time I lifted the covers from my head, the sun was already setting. I peeked over at my phone to see the time. Five twenty p.m. Great, I thought. I'd managed to sleep the whole day away over a guy I'd only known for about two weeks. Looking at my phone a little longer, I also noticed several missed texts— from my Three Rs + a J WhatsApp message chain, my parents, and Olivia. I decided to check Liv's first, thinking it was probably going to be the one with the least chance of making me throw my phone across the room. I was sure the girls wanted to know about last night with Zayn, since I'd foolishly texted them while we were at crazy golf to declare that I wanted him to spend the night. And my parents? Well, there was no telling what their texts said, but they had the best chance of saying something that would make me cringe and groan my way back under the covers.

Opening Olivia's text chain, I almost immediately regretted my decision.

Hey babes. I know you're probably out with that sexy singer of yours but hit me back and let me know if you're free tonight, yeah.

I looked closely at her first text and noticed she had originally sent me the message around noon. Two hours later, she'd texted again.

Okay, but are you two tied up, eh? Or maybe you're at one of your afternoon teas again?

Still with no response from me, she texted again another hour later.

Rob? You're all right, eh? It's not like you to go ghost.

Well, this was going to go well, I thought. It had been five hours since her first text and two since her last. There was no way I was getting out of responding without telling her about my latest dating misfortune. I sucked up my pride and responded back.

Hey, Liv, sorry babe. I've been in bed all day.

Olivia: What?! All day? What gives? Oh wait, like, in a good way?

No, definitely not in a good way.

Olivia: Oh damn, what's wrong?

Well, Zayn broke up with me this morning.

Olivia: Not sexy singer?!

Yep. So, he can lose the fun nickname now, I suppose.

Every time Liv typed "sexy singer" in the past, I could literally hear it in her British accent, sounding more like *seggzy singah*. Normally, this sent me through the roof with laughter, but today it just felt cruel, and I needed her to stop. Thankfully, she took the cue.

Olivia: Did he say why, babe?

Honestly, Liv, it's a long story.

   Well, actually, I corrected myself, it's a pretty short story.

The same short story as always for me. He just wasn't that into me.

Olivia: Nooo, that can't be true. I saw you two together. He was very into you, babe. Like, very.

Yeah, but that was before Samaya, his childhood friend, professed her love to him, by text, while we were in each other's arms. I can't exactly compete with that.

Olivia: Oh my God, Rob. WTF.

I know.

Olivia: Okay, you know what? You're coming over tonight. It's what I was texting you about anyways, but we can just change the vibe some.

No, no, I really don't want to do anything.

Olivia: It's not a request, yeah? Get up. Take a shower. Throw some whatever clothes on. And bring your butt to The City.

Sigh, that feels so far away right now, Liv.

Olivia: I won't take this time to tell you that you shouldn't be living in Westminster anyway because who the heck lives in Westminster. That would be mean, and I'm being nice right now, but I'm certainly not letting you use that as an excuse.

Oh yes, you're the epitome of nice, I texted back, finally finding a laugh still somewhere deep in my soul.

Olivia: Exactly. Even with your sarcasm. Now, get up. Chop chop. I'll have everything ready by the time you get to me.

Liv.

Olivia: Trust me, babe. I got you.

I put down my phone and stayed on my back for a while, going over all that had happened in my head. With my eyes closed, I visualized every laugh I'd shared with Zayn and every touch that had sent shivers down my spine, trying to figure out how I'd missed the biggest gotcha of all—a man in love with someone else. Over and over, I recalled each moment that we spent together, and still, nothing triggered alarms until that text. Or maybe it was the sister, or even just the fact that I'd started letting my guard down with him at all.

After a few minutes passed, I sat up again, determined to try to pull myself together to make it to Liv's. It wasn't like I'd fallen in love with the guy, I thought to myself. We'd only just met. And yet, every time I tried to explain it away, the pain that I felt seemed impenetrable. Maybe not even because of Zayn himself, but after all the times I'd been lied to, ghosted, stood up, treated like a trophy, cheated on and even adored in secret, I'd foolishly thought things had a chance of being different this time. It was like someone who perpetually burned themselves on a hot stove; at some point, I had to look in the mirror and see that it was me.

With another internal push, I finally stood up next to my bed—the first time I'd done so all day. Then I straightened my comforter, took a deep breath and forced myself to start moving, one foot in front of the other. I'd almost made it out my room to go to the bathroom when I noticed my reflection in the bedroom mirror and stopped to look at myself. When I'd first moved in, I thought having a mirror in each room was a blessing. Now, looking at the woman who stood before me—a disheveled version of myself, dressed in a white tank top and gray shorts with one knee-high sock that had dropped down to my ankle and my blond highlights twisting themselves out of the messy bun I'd put my hair in the night before—I was ashamed. My night scarf that protected my edges had long since fallen off in the bed, acting as a sort of symbol to how I felt in the moment—scattered, forgotten and unloved—

and nothing in the mirror reminded me of the woman I knew myself to be.

I stood there for another few minutes, waiting, hoping to somehow see something different. Something that could make me believe all the heartbreak was ultimately worth it and that I was going to be stronger and better in the end. It took a while, longer than I wanted it to, but eventually, as I watched my chest rise and fall, I was reminded that the beaten-up heart within it was the very same one keeping me alive and giving her all to the people around her. No matter how many times she was hurt and disappointed, that heart managed to rally, I realized. And sure, I was tired of learning lessons when it came to dating, but I was still here. Christine had ultimately taught me the importance of that. And so as much as I wanted to just stop trying, stop dating, stop putting myself out there to get crushed over and over again, I refused to let Chrissy or myself down.

With one last inhale in, I closed my eyes and felt the flicker of a fire start to return inside me. I was still here. And despite what I saw in that mirror, the Robin Johnson who'd come all the way to London to build a new life really only needed a hot shower, some lip gloss, a bit of edge control and a couple spins of Mimi to get ready to take on the world again. Or, at the very least, put on a brave face for girls' night in at Liv's.

I walked back to my phone, texted Olivia that I was jumping in the shower and then dragged my fingers right to the playlist I needed to hear the most: *The Emancipation of Mimi*. With another quick swipe, I scrolled down to "One and Only" and let the smooth

sounds begin playing in my room as I danced my way
to my closet to look for the perfect pick-me-up outfit—
something casual but oh so cute to remind myself and
the world I wasn't done yet.

Chapter Eleven

"Yes! You made it," said Olivia as she swung open her front door to let me in.

Greeting me with the kind of smile I desperately needed—big, genuine and specific to me—she took my coat and stopped to snicker as we both immediately noticed the differences in our outfits for the night. Liv, who had explicitly told me to put on what she called "whatever clothes," stood in front of me wearing an oversize T-shirt, a pair of gray biker shorts and fuzzy slippers. In contrast, I'd come over in a matching two-piece nude pink lounge set complete with knit joggers and a crop-top tank. In my defense, it was a very comfy and cute outfit—I'd thought perfect for a stylish girls'-night-in affair. Clearly, I'd misread the invitation a little.

"Were you wondering if I would?" I asked, stepping into her hallway.

"Honestly, I had a fifty-fifty bet going with myself on whether you'd text me some absolutely ridiculous reason for not coming, like your dog ate your keys and you just couldn't very well leave your flat now, you know."

"The dog I don't have," I said, giggling at the way her brain worked.

"Like I said, it was going to be a fantastical excuse if you came up with one, but you didn't! You came."

Liv's smile continued lighting up her face even as she paused to hang up my coat in her front closet. Meanwhile, I slipped off my shoes and closed the door behind me.

"You might not know this about me yet, Liv, but I'm a woman of my word," I said. "I wouldn't say I was coming and then flake."

"You didn't actually say yes, though, right?"

Liv turned back to me and stared at me with a mischievous smirk as I suddenly realized she was spot-on. She'd totally finished our conversation before I ever even had a chance to say no, and yet there I was, standing in her flat despite my initial attempt at a protest. Tricky, tricky.

"Fair," I said. "But now I know your MO."

"Whateva. It got you here. That's all that matters."

As we walked farther into her apartment, my nose caught the distinct whiff of baked mozzarella cheese and tomato sauce. It could only be one thing, I surmised. I just hoped that she'd picked something up to par, even if it could likely never live up to Lou Malnati's sausage-and-spinach pizza in Chicago.

"Did you get what I think you did?" I asked, rubbing my fingers together in anticipation.

Olivia didn't say another word, just grinned and raised her eyebrows twice as if to imply *yes* as she turned and kept walking into her partially lit living room. I dutifully followed behind her and moments later found myself staring in awe at the full-on immaculate spread laid out on her rounded silver coffee table, somehow spotlighted by the end table lamp that only offered enough light so that it was possible to see each other in the room. There, presented with tons of confetti and balloons and silverware, was an extra-large, brick-oven baked margarita pizza, a gallon-size crystal bowl of doubly buttered popcorn and at least three bottles of prosecco.

"I'm sorry, are we expecting more people tonight?" I asked. "Like, is this a real party?"

"No," she said sheepishly. "I kind of started putting things together and then couldn't stop myself. First it was the confetti, which I randomly found while I was pulling out the champagne flutes. And then I remembered I had balloons, and I thought they might help cheer you up—so, I don't know, here we are."

"Honestly, Liv, I love it," I replied, drawing closer to the coffee table so that I could see more of the intricacies of her spread. Not only had she tossed colorful confetti everywhere, but somehow it seemed to perfectly match the champagne flutes that were embellished with stunning pink jewels. I guessed that was why she'd found them near each other. Either way, it was quite the surprise treat, and it would certainly be used in the future as an example of her ability to be just as outlandish as me if she ever tried to say otherwise. What were friends good for if we couldn't pre-plan jokes about each other, after all.

Olivia watched with equal glee and anticipation as I carefully inspected the pizza with my eyes, trying to see if it would live up to my high expectations.

"Obviously, it's not a deep-dish pizza," she remarked. "But I promise, it's really, really good. Probably some of the best I've had in London."

"That's high praise, Olivia."

"I know. Maybe I shouldn't have set myself up like that," she said with a smile.

"It's quite all right. I mean, you've outdone yourself tonight already. So, if the pizza is like a six out of ten, it'll be okay."

"Don't lie—no, it won't be!"

"Okay, it might not be, but I wouldn't say otherwise."

We both laughed and finally began moving toward the sofa to have a seat. Liv immediately plopped down onto the hunter green couch cushions, folding her legs underneath her. Then she leaned toward the coffee table again, gesturing at some of the other items in front of us.

"One other thing. I know you love your prosecco punch, but I didn't have time to get any pomegranates, so I figured just a couple chilled glasses would have to do for tonight."

Wait, I hadn't realized the flutes were chilled, too. I picked up one to test it out, and sure enough, it was cool to the touch. I was definitely going to use this against her—good-naturedly, of course—in the future.

"Okay, honestly, you have bejeweled chilled flutes," I said, placing my glass back down onto the table and joining her on the left side of the couch. "We're not exactly slumming it by not having pomegranates."

"Well, my fancy American friend was coming over, so I had to bring out what you all call the fine china, you know," Liv said, smiling in jest.

"Please!"

"Whateva, babe. Protest all you want, but you know it's true. That's why you're sitting on my couch right now, wearing a matching two-piece set for girls' night in. I couldn't very well have you show up here and all I had was some greasy pizza and paper plates. No!"

"This isn't casual?" I said looking down at my outfit and ignoring the rest of her comment. "I didn't wear the open cardigan that came with it!"

Olivia fell face forward into her couch cushions.

"Oh my God!" she said with her voice only slightly muffled by her couch cushions. "You're so adorable. Truly."

"Well, listen," I said, shrugging my shoulders and picking up one of the prosecco bottles to open it. "I may be heartbroken, but I don't have to look like it."

"Now, that's the truth!"

I flashed back to my image in the mirror and shuddered at what came to my mind. I hated that I'd let a guy bring me to that point, but at least it hadn't been for long. If it was one thing that I knew I had going for myself, it was that I never let the hurt linger too long. That just wasn't how Lawrence and Sharon Johnson raised me.

Liv waited until I'd opened the bottle of prosecco before she quickly swiped it out of my hand so that she could be the one controlling the pours. Carefully, she picked up each glass and tipped the bottle on a slant as the sparkling wine rushed out. Then she waited patiently until the bubbles died down to add more, doing her routine at least twice for each glass until she'd filled them to the tops. Once done, she raised her glass so that I could meet hers in the air.

"And speaking of heartbreaks," she began.

"Wait, we're not about to toast to heartbreaks, are we?"

"*Nooo.* We're toasting to getting over heartbreaks the best way I know how—with food, drinks, lots of laughs and cheesy British romcoms."

"Okay, yes! Just checking. Cheers to that!" I shouted out, much louder than I'd intended. But Liv's declaration suddenly reminded me of home—not the physical one, but the one made with love because of my best friends—and the joy poured out of me like the champagne just a moment before. They would have loved a night in like tonight, I thought. Balloons and all.

"You're going to so enjoy my friends when they come in April," I said in between sips. "You all share pretty similar heartbreak philosophies."

"I can't wait," Olivia remarked, leaning back into her couch with a slice of pizza in one hand and her glass in the other. "Besides, if they helped you bring you to me in any way, they're already some of my faves."

She took a large gulp of her drink, finishing off the glass so she could pick up her remote control.

"Now, let's get to the brass tacks."

Liv spoke with intention, looking at me with a very serious expression, completely contrary to what her demeanor had been since I walked in the door.

"What's first on our showing? *Bridget Jones's Diary* or the reboot of *Four Weddings and a Funeral*?"

We both paused for a beat and glanced at each other with a knowing look.

"*Bridget,*" we said in unison and then burst out laughing.

"Right? I mean, what other classic could we watch at a time such as this?" I asked.

"You're right. There is none better, babe."

Olivia pressed the play button on her remote, and the all-too-familiar sounds of Renée Zellweger's opening monologue about being single once again at thirty-two on New Year's Day began blaring from her TV. I could instantly relate, even if there were some key differences—not the least of which were our choices in style.

"At least you're not heading to your family's turkey curry buffet alone," Liv said, stuffing a handful of buttered popcorn into her mouth as she tried not to snort from her giggles. "And you'd certainly never get caught dead in Bridget's carpet of an outfit."

"Too soon, Olivia! Too soon," I responded, joining her in laughter.

She was right, though. As much as it felt like my heart had been ripped out of my body once again, stomped on and given to *Samaya*, I wasn't quite as bad off as our dear movie protagonist. I *could* see my parents trying to set me up with any random loser who had a nice job and a 401(k) if I came home single one more time, however.

We continued watching in amusement and horror as the movie played on, using our glasses as microphones for loudly singing along to "All by Myself" with Bridget and Jamie O'Neal and fully relating to her comical resolutions to do better in all aspects of her life. I particularly understood how easily Bridget completely disregarded every single one of these plans the moment Hugh Grant flashed his charming smile in her face. I mean, what woman wouldn't say *screw it* and then screw Daniel instead? Not this one, that was for sure.

As Bridget embarrassed herself on stage, blabbering on about whether someone was the greatest author of all time, I looked over at Liv and relaxed my body into her sofa, finally realizing that I hadn't needed to put on a happy mask at all to spend time with her tonight. As it turned out, unlike my horrible luck at dating, I'd managed to find an actual, genuine friend in my new country. That was certainly nothing to sneeze at.

I grabbed another slice of pizza and held back laughter tears watching Bridget squeeze into her panty-like shapewear, knowing all too well the conflict of wanting to wear the thing that would at once smooth out your fat rolls and make you look good enough to eat but then also make it look like you had on granny under-wear should someone actually try to take a bite of you. Having seen *Bridget Jones's Diary* no fewer than sixty times already, I knew that we'd eventually get to the point in the movie where we all knew Daniel was a jerk with few redeemable qualities. But oh, how my heart swelled with joy watching him joke around upon see-ing her, as he called them, "enormous pants" and still wanting to completely devour her. That was the kind of unbridled passion I wanted in my next relationship.

"I, too, wear pretty big pants!" said an unnamed deep voice from Liv's doorway, causing me to nearly jump out of my skin.

I turned to look at Olivia and noticed that while she looked highly annoyed, she wasn't at all terrified like I would be if a man's voice just randomly popped up out of nowhere in the darkness of the apartment that I lived in alone.

"Ugh, what are you doing here?" she asked, scream-ing out into the direction of her hallway. "I'm sorry, it's my brother," she said under her breath toward me.

Great, I thought. Just what I needed. Another un-expected sibling encounter just a day after the last one had rocked my world.

"A brother can't drop by to see his sister anymore?" asked the intruder.

From the darkness of her hallway, Liv's brother fi-nally appeared to us, having removed his shoes and stepping into the living room with his perfectly straight white teeth beaming in the backlight of the TV. He looked to be about six feet tall, with gorgeous cocoa-brown skin, intensely dark eyes, a slight beard and a low-top haircut with tapered sides. His broad shoulders and bulging upper-arm muscles were only somewhat concealed by the unbuttoned denim shirt that was rolled up to his elbows and simultaneously revealed a crisp white T-shirt underneath. With that, he'd paired some slim-fit jeans with one knee exposed and a thin gold chain that fell just at the lower part of his very climbable chest.

All told, he was as handsome and captivating as I'd pictured when Liv first mentioned him—which meant that whatever happened tonight, I needed to make sure I didn't end up starting to like him. Everything about this guy, from the playful smile he had on his face to the way he looked like he could scoop me up with no problems, spelled trouble.

"What's the world coming to?" he asked Liv, walking into the room and noticing the decorations, the coffee table spread and me all at once. He locked eyes with me with a quizzical look on his face. "Something I need to know, sister? Are you on a date? Does David know?"

"No, this is my friend from work. We're just having girls' night in, but I went a little overboard with the setup," she replied, sort of slinking into the corner of her sofa.

"Don't downplay yourself like that," I chimed in, looking at her and trying to see where my totally unashamed friend went to that quickly. Was this a sibling thing, I wondered? Or something Craig did to her?

"I'm not," she said in protest and then looked back

at her brother. "Not saying my production was a bad thing, but just that...no, it's not for a date."

"All right," he said, shrugging his shoulders and walking farther into the living room.

"But obviously I'm still not alone," she added. "You might want to call or at least knock before coming in next time, yeah? As you so eloquently mentioned, I do have a whole boyfriend. What if we'd been having sex or something?"

"Oh, do you and David have sex? You don't really give me that vibe. Plus, what's the point of you giving me keys if I have to knock?"

"I hate you, I swear."

"No, you don't. You could never."

Craig's smile widened as he grabbed a slice of pizza and took a huge bite, letting some of the cheese drizzle down his lips before licking it up. He clearly knew that he was annoying his sister but also seemed to be enjoying it. And despite her complaints, she wasn't exactly asking him to leave. As he took another bite, he turned his attention back to me, and I instinctively, despite not really wanting to, met his eyes. It was as if something was drawing me toward him—maybe it was the fact that he was eating my heartbreak pizza or maybe, worst-case scenario, there was something inherently addictive about the way he seemed to stare into my soul without even trying.

Almost finished with his first slice, Craig grabbed another and moved toward us again like a man completely undeterred by any thought that he was interrupting something he couldn't join in. Then, almost exactly like Liv had done before, he plopped his full weight down into the sofa, managing to take up much of the space in between me and her. Clearly, I gathered, in his eyes, I was actually the odd man out. This was his sister and her couch, and he was completely used to making himself comfortable on it on a late Saturday evening.

Once he was fully settled in, I looked down and noticed that our thighs were so close to each other they were almost but not quite touching. And yet, unless I was completely losing touch with reality, I could see how, with just the right *accidental* move, we'd have no option but to be glued together. The guy was good, I realized. Charming in a sort of unassuming way, but where any woman looking for the signs would instantly know what he was doing. After all, it wasn't like he sat down and immediately put his arms around me, but he'd positioned himself so undeniably close that he'd know instantly if there was any sort of chemistry between us before he ever made a move. What I hated even more about his ploy was that it had worked; the goose bumps rising on my arms clearly signaled to us both that I was more than a little interested in knowing what his touch would feel like.

With an intentional pause in his chewing, Craig dragged his eyes from my thighs up to my stomach then to my arms—lingering just long enough there to let me know he noticed the tiny prickly bumps making an appearance—casually glided them over my chest, then to my neck, my lips and ultimately to my eyes. It took less than a minute, but it felt like he'd somehow taken in enough to memorize every part of my body for later. And when he was done with his assessment, he leaned over to me and dropped his voice to give his best attempt at a whisper as if he wanted to tell me a secret.

"I'm Craig," he said, his Brixton accent sounding thicker than it had when he'd initially walked in.

"She knows who you are, dummy," Liv said from her side of the couch. "If you're done trying to seduce my friend, I still would like to know why you're here."

Liv picked up the bottle of prosecco again and poured herself another glass before guzzling it back. Craig barely acknowledged her statement, casually poking her with his right hand while he kept his eyes on me, waiting for me to say something in response to his introduction.

"I'm Robin," I answered.

By this point, I too wanted to know why he'd stopped by unannounced, and it seemed like neither of us was going to get a proper response until I indulged him on what he wanted to know about me: who was this strange woman his sister had gone all out for but whom he'd never met.

"*Robinnnn,*" Craig responded, elongating my name with his tongue as he said it aloud.

The way it reverberated off his lips, I could have been locked in an echo chamber just listening to him say my name for hours and been in deep ecstasy.

"Oh, right," he said, realization finally showing on his face. "Liv's new American friend!"

"Don't act like you didn't know that when I said my

friend from work earlier," said Liv, trying to get her brother's attention again.

"I can't keep up with all your friends, man," Craig responded, still without looking her way.

He leaned in closer to me and whispered again. "Between you and me, I think she believes you all are besties or something."

"We're getting there," I replied with a giggle that came from somewhere deep inside before I could stop it. "For one, she tricked me into come here to eat and laugh my sorrows away tonight. That's bestie behavior if I know it."

"Yeah, that's what you interrupted, bruv."

Craig leaned back into the sofa, positioning himself so that he could easily turn to Liv or me with a quick swivel of his head. Then he spread his arms out wide on the tops of the back sofa cushions, his hands landing on either side of me and Liv's shoulders.

"Well, any bestie of Liv's must also be my BFF forever," he said, lightly mocking us. "Isn't that right, dear sister?"

Liv groaned off to the right of him and returned his poke from earlier, landing hers in his waist. I could tell she was still frustrated that he'd interrupted our movie night, but she also seemed to be growing more and more concerned as he refused to answer her question.

"You *still* haven't told me what you brought you here tonight," she said, her once-jovial tone conveying to us all that she was now serious and needed an answer sooner than later.

"Truthfully," Craig, said with a sigh, now presumably ready to spill his guts as he looked at his sister with a vulnerability that I hadn't thought possible, given his behavior since arriving, "I had another awful date just now, and I thought you might be able to remind me that I'm not some horrible person who's destined to die alone."

Unable to control myself, I burst out laughing from my side of our sad little couch of misfits. It was one of those laughs that started as a small giggle but then grew until I couldn't contain the noise coming from my mouth, snorts and all.

"What's that about?" Craig asked Liv with a concerned expression. "I just poured my heart out, yeah, and your girl's cracking up?"

"She's laughing because she's here for the same thing," Liv said matter-of-factly.

"I got dumped this morning by a guy whose childhood best friend told him that she loved him while we were on a date last night," I added, attempting to explain my amusement as tears trickled down my face from laughing so hard. "And the guy before him had such whiplash mood swings on our date, I thought I was on a roller-coaster ride at Six Flags in America. The one before him professed his love to me, on a first date, after drinking too much with only tea sandwiches on his stomach. And before all that, I had a prince completely enamored with me, but I threw it all away because I foolishly believed I deserved better. Than a prince!"

"Wait, when did you date a prince?" Liv asked from her side of the couch.

"And which one?" Craig added.

"That's not the point," I said, grabbing the bottle of prosecco and my bejeweled flute to pour myself another glass.

"That's a pretty good point," argued Craig.

"Yeah, and how did I not know about this before?" Liv asked in return.

"No, no, it's not the point, I promise."

I took a long sip before continuing.

"The point is when it comes to dating, I am apparently a masochist. I even had one guy in America tell me that he, a Black man, didn't believe the trans-Atlantic slave trade happened. And this was while we were on a date at the Smithsonian National Museum of African American History and Culture!"

"That's a really long name," Liv muttered under her breath.

"It is," I said quickly agreeing. "But also, not the point. You see, you two, you may not know this, but you are sitting next to the champion of disastrous dates. I am the woman who managed to date so many men in DC that, seven years after a date went so badly with one guy that I nicknamed him Freddy Krueger in my phone, I met him again, forgot that we knew each other before and went on a second horrible date with him! And don't get me started about how hard it can be to find a man confident enough to stand next to a woman who is five-nine and loves wearing three-inch heels just as much as I enjoy rocking a pair of Chucks. It's maddening! So yeah, I am laughing. I'm sorry, I shouldn't be laughing, but I am, at the fact that *you* think you're the one destined to die alone when, clearly, it's me. I'm the one who gets to hold that title."

"And this is why we're having girls' night in," Liv helpfully explained as I caught my breath and stuffed some buttered popcorn into my mouth.

"And watching *Bridget Jones's Diary*." Craig nodded, the realization of his surroundings—pizza, popcorn, prosecco and romcom movie blaring from the TV—making that much more sense to him now.

"Yes, exactly," I muffled out with popcorn still in my mouth. "So, really, I guess it's fate you came by tonight. You get to see what a real disaster looks like. And now you can go home, confident in the knowledge that whatever you think you are, you're not quite at my level yet."

Craig shifted his body, turning to face me even while still seated. With the same deeply intense eyes that I'd noticed when he walked in, but now combined with the sensitivity he'd shown with Liv, he pulled my attention toward him and refused to let it go as he traced his eyes over my face.

"I don't see anything close to a disaster in front of me," he said. "And just so you know, you could wear six-inch heels and I'd be perfectly content looking up into your eyes all night."

I dropped my head quickly, unable to fully digest that kind of compliment when I'd just spent all day agonizing over losing someone else. With that motion, one of my curls fell into my face, and without prompting, Craig gently moved it to the side so that he could see me in full again. Then, carefully, he placed his hand very lightly under my chin and raised my head back up to meet his gaze.

"You know what else I see? A beautiful—no, stunning—woman who's been hurt a lot, but she's probably so used to winning in all the other areas of her life. So, she's trying her damnedest to not give up on love…even it's hard sometimes. And so, sometimes, she makes very long, very elaborate jokes to keep from crying."

Craig's words penetrated something deep inside me, and I looked back at him in wonder at how he could glean so much about me after only having just met me. I also hated how entranced I seemed to be by him when every bone in my body was telling me to get up, say my thanks to Liv and get out as fast as I could. My heart, though, that stubborn beast of a girl who'd awakened in the mirror earlier, wouldn't let me move.

No, she wanted me to allow myself to get lost in the reverberations of Craig's deep, velvet voice as he spoke to me, about me, like he could see something so many others missed—*the real Robin*. Just the thought of that sent flutters through my chest, causing me to lose my breath for just long enough that when I caught it again, I let out a deep sigh in his direction.

"That's quite the read," I finally responded.

"I call it like I see it," he said, tilting his head and clearing his throat before pivoting back to his argument. When he spoke again, he made sure to lift his volume back up to address the whole room. His tone was also back to the casual arrogance that somehow made him frustratingly attractive.

"But either way, as fantastical as your stories have been, and they *have* been—I haven't forgotten about the prince—it doesn't mean you get to hold the trophy on being the one to die alone."

Craig leaned back again into his wide-seated position on the sofa and turned to silently get Liv to back up his position. When she only returned his glare with a casual toss of her hand in defeat, his face gave away the acknowledgment that he finally had to fully reveal what made his date so awful if he was going to try to take the crown from me.

"If you want to hear a proper dating fiasco, let me recount for you how I just came from dinner with a woman who spent the entire night canoodling with me, telling me all she wanted to do later in the evening and ordering two hundred quid worth of food—with takeaway. And then right as we were walking to my car, her boyfriend pulled up. I stood there like an idiot in disbelief as she gleefully climbed into his car and waved goodbye to me—from this man's lap."

"Oh Craig, no, what?!" Liv screamed out.

"I know. It must be karma from all the times—"

"When, what, you weren't exactly honest with the women you were dating, either?" I asked, interrupting him with an *oh yes, Liv told me about you* look on my face.

"Liv!"

Craig shifted his position again, this time to look directly at his sister, and she meekly shrugged her shoulders before picking up a slice of pizza.

"Well, anyway," he said, shaking his head at her and

then spinning it back to me, "yes, maybe it's that. But regardless of the reason, and my karma, I think I need a night of romcoms just as much as the two of you... you especially, Liv, since nothing's actually wrong with your relationship except that it's bloody boring."

"Now's not the time," she said, rolling her eyes with a mouthful of pizza.

"It's true," Craig responded matter-of-factly.

"Whateva!"

Now Craig tried to get me on his side as he turned in my direction for a cosign.

"I haven't actually met David yet, so I can't say," I offered in my defense.

"Well, that should tell you everything you need to know right there."

"She just met you, too, you know," Liv said as she wiped her hands down her shirt.

"Yeah, and not a moment too soon. You all clearly needed me here tonight."

Liv fell back into her side of the sofa in exasperation, and I smiled, watching the dynamic between her and her brother. It was clearly one full of love, if also annoyance, in only the way a younger brother could elicit.

"So, say we let you stay," I jumped in to get the conversation past the state of Olivia and David's relationship. She hadn't yet mentioned any problems to me about it, so I didn't want to make her feel like she was being put on the spot. "You have to promise not to be one of those guys who spends the whole time just making fun of the movies. We're going to lovingly roast some moments from time to time, but ultimately..."

"You need to be reminded in the beauty of happily-ever-afters," he interjected. "I get it. I'm the proud younger brother of a romcom fanatic, so I may just have watched this movie even more than you have."

Craig lifted his eyes toward me as if he was offering a friendly challenge that I wasn't quite ready to accept. Still caught off guard by our interaction just moments before, I instead tried to reposition myself in my corner of the couch, both in an attempt to avoid his ever-direct gaze and to curl my toes underneath me as some sort of comfort mechanism. Despite my best efforts, however, nothing seemed to sway his attention from me as he somehow kept his eyes in place, waiting for the moment he knew I'd return to them. Which I eventually did, to my growing horror.

As soon as Craig locked his eyes with mine again, he continued.

"Plus, I also know there's no better scene than when Darcy tells Bridget that he likes her just…as…she is."

He spoke his last few words slowly, letting them linger in the air between us. And while I knew he was, of course, just reciting the lines from the movie, inside it felt as if he was speaking them directly to me. Or maybe I just secretly wanted him to.

"Oh, all right, you've made your case long enough," Liv said, breaking the concentrated stare between the two of us and, I'm sure, in an attempt to cool down the heat growing in her living room. "What do you say, Rob? Can he stay?"

She raised her eyebrow at me for good measure, slanting her body upward so that I could see her past

Craig's imposing stature between us. I couldn't tell if she was letting me know that whatever I decided she would go along with or not. What I did know, though, was that this aching in the pit of my chest wasn't going to let him leave anytime soon—even if every other part of me was still trying to fight it.

"Yeah, Rob? What do you say?" Craig asked, interjecting himself once again into our thing and emphasizing his use of my once-rarely-used nickname as he poked out his lower lip to plead his case.

"Fine. Any man who knows the third best scene in *Bridget Jones's Diary* can stay as long as he wants as far as I'm concerned," I responded, smirking and shaking off the brief thought I had of using that lower lip for other purposes.

"Third best?!" Craig said, repeating my phrasing with utter disgust. "Liv, you invited this woman into your home with wildly ridiculous takes like this?"

He paused dramatically and then, with a sigh, turned my way again and flashed that adorable—ugh—smile of his.

"Okay, it's all right. I won't judge. Tell me, what are the first two…in your opinion?"

"The enormous panties scene that you rudely walked in on," I offered in retort.

"Okay, fair."

"And obviously, the best scene of all is when Bridget goes running out of her apartment to try to apologize to Mark about what was in her diary only to find out he was simply buying her a new one so they could have a fresh start."

"That's not fair. You can't pick the last scene in a romcom as your favorite," Craig protested.

"Why can't I?"

"That's the ultimate cheat code! C'mon, the happy ending?!"

"We're watching it because we want the happy ending!"

"Yeah, but it's all the great moments before then that make it so sweet. Liv, tell her."

Craig turned his head to his sister, looking for her to once again be on his side.

"Oh no, I'm staying out of this," she said, throwing up her hands and laughing at the two of us.

"That's code for she agrees with me but doesn't want to say so because you girls are supposed to stick together or whatever."

We all looked over at the TV, at once realizing that Liv had never paused the movie and that Craig's favorite moment was about to come up. With a flash, he picked up the remote control in one hand, grabbing my hand with his other as he turned the volume up. And there I sat, watching in pure awe as this super-charming, funny and slightly cocky guy recited Mark Darcy's iconic speech to Bridget at the bottom of her friend's steps. When it was nearing the end, Craig twisted himself toward me again and raised his voice just slightly more than before to ensure I could hear him over the TV.

"In fact, despite appearances," he said, peering deeply into my eyes, "Robin, I like you very much."

As Bridget jokingly clarified Mark's statement by

pointing out all the things he'd mentioned were wrong about her and her life choices on the screen, I stared back in amazement at the fact that Craig had taken my breath away once again just by adding my name into a monologue I'd heard a million times over. He also hadn't let my hand go but had drawn it up to his chest so that I could feel the flutter of his heart beating while he looked at me.

"I like you very much. Just as you are," he said along with the movie.

Craig then brought his lips to within inches of my neck, suddenly causing me to forget, just for a second, that we were sitting right next to his sister, my friend. The room was deafeningly quiet as the movie contin- ued playing. And in the still of those moments, Craig lifted his head so that his lips dragged along the curve of my chin. The only thing that saved me from com- plete destruction was the interruption of Liv clearing her throat.

"And to think, I worried about you two meeting at first," she remarked with a giggle.

Craig slowly leaned away from me and placed his back into the sofa once again, running one hand down his face to compose himself but keeping the other in- tertwined with mine.

"Sorry, sis," he said, briefly turning to Liv for the shortest of apologies before looking my way again. "Still think it's only third best?" he asked with a grin.

"You may be right," I relented. "I'm willing to say it's better than the granny panties scene, for now. But it's still not as iconic as the diary scene. I mean it's called *Bridget Jones's Diary*, for goodness' sake."

"Okay, I'll give you that…for now," Craig said, cleverly using my cadence and phrasing against me. "The good thing is I've got all night to convince you otherwise."

From somewhere deep inside, a smile formed on my lips, and I was suddenly desperately thankful for the dim lighting in Liv's living room. Despite the nagging voice in my head, I really liked the thought of spending the rest of the night watching movies with Craig and Olivia, even if I was still trying to decide just how much trouble I was getting myself into by holding the hand of a man who readily acknowledged that he'd been less than truthful with past girlfriends. As we all turned our attention back to the movie, I rested my head on the back cushions, placing it ever so slightly closer to Craig—taking a page right out of his book from earlier.

I heard him take in a deep breath and watched his chest lift up slightly before he tightened his clutch on my hand. If my plan had been to avoid being swept up by Liv's brother, I'd massively failed. And the thing was, there was no turning back from it now. I just had to hope the stove somehow wouldn't burn me again.

"And we still have to hear this prince story before the end of the night," Liv said off to the side of us. "I'm not letting whatever this is going on with you two distract me from that."

"She's right, you know," Craig said, turning his

head so that he had direct eye contact with me again. "There's no way you're getting away…without telling us all the gory royal family details."

Part 3

"Have enough courage to trust love one more time and always one more time."

—Maya Angelou

Chapter Twelve

"I can't believe you're going out with my brother today."

"I know," I said, pausing my desperate room search for the cobalt blue, long-sleeve crop top I wanted to wear with my faded denim overalls to make eye contact with Liv through the FaceTime app on my laptop. "And low-key, I'm actually kind of nervous."

"Really? I couldn't tell," she responded, her voice dripping with sarcasm. "You needn't be, though. I can tell you from firsthand experience watching the two of you on my couch the other night that my brother is way, way into you."

"You do recall that you also thought Zayn was super into me, right? Because of the same firsthand experience with us at the nightclub?"

Liv scrunched her face and shook her head in reply as I resumed my search, picking up, inspecting and then tossing clothes back into their respective rejection piles now labeled in my head *not the thing I'm looking for.*

"Okay, so I was off once."

"And you are the very same person who told me that your brother was bad news."

"Ugh, I did say that, too, didn't I?"

"Mmm-hmm. So, do you want to ask me again why I'm nervous?"

"No, I guess not," Liv said, rolling her eyes.

I caught her just out of my periphery as I picked up something else blue and realized yet again it wasn't the top I wanted. In response, I tilted my head back toward her, lifted my eyes and pursed my lips to make a smacking sound, all meant to convey one thing: *you know I'm right, girl.*

"If it helps, things are…different, though…since I made that statement back when we first met up for drinks."

I paused again and doubled back to face Olivia in the camera upon hearing the hesitation in her voice.

"Different how? What aren't you telling me?"

"Well, Craig might kill me for saying this, but he's actually been seeing a therapist lately, and I don't know—I'm starting to see a change even in how open he is. Like, obviously, he's still working on stuff, but you saw it the other night—in between all the jokes and overly charming sarcasm, he got a little vulnerable sometimes, too."

"Yeah, I think that's what ultimately convinced me to give him a shot," I said, recalling how we'd spent hours laughing and watching movies at Liv's last weekend. And maybe also the way my insides warmed when Craig looked at me.

"*Sooo*...that gives me a little hope for him and for you, too," she said with a shrug. "You never know. I just, you know, maybe don't need to see it in my face all the time."

"That's totally fair. And actually, I've been meaning to check in and ask if this is too weird for you. Because if it is, I can just call him and tell him we can't go there. Your friendship is worth too much to me to mess things up over a guy...even one as handsome and charming as Craig."

"No, please, it's not weird at all. I would tell you. Trust me."

"Okay, good," I said, pivoting to begin looking for my shirt again. "Because honestly, I'm really looking forward to today. If I could just find this damn shirt!"

"What is it that you're so desperate to find, anyway?" she asked. "You have a million tops that would look cute with overalls. Why do you need this one so badly?"

Before I could respond, out of the corner of my eye, I saw what looked to be my hidden treasure, buried underneath the pile of clean but unfolded laundry sitting on the lavender tufted trunk in front of my bed. I moved in close and was pleasantly surprised to see, after having picked up that same pile four times before, I was right. It had been there all along.

"Yes!" I screamed out and twirled around my room, waving my achievement in my hand.

Finally, I turned my attention at least partially back to Liv to answer the question that had lingered as I explored my room like a freakin' detective on a mission.

"Okay, I know this is going to sound wacky," I started saying as I inspected the top to see if it needed ironing or if it would properly stretch out enough once I put it on. "But I had a dream where I was in this outfit on my date with Craig, and it was *sooo* beautiful and peaceful that I literally woke up with a smile on my face. And I just figured, if nothing else, that was a sign for what I should wear today."

"All right," she replied, trying not to giggle too loudly. "What else happened in this incredible dream of yours? Wait—maybe don't tell me. I'm not sure how much I can handle yet."

Liv squirmed in her seat as she awaited my reply. Unbeknownst to her, however, she didn't have anything to worry about as far as me saying anything sexual to her. The dream hadn't gone that far. It really was just a genuinely nice date.

"Don't worry," I assured her. "The only shocking thing that happened was that I was on time."

"Whoa. That is big. Did the date start at work?"

I laughed while wiggling myself into the crop top to see if it would work as I'd pictured. Once on, I stepped to the floor-length mirror in my bedroom, buckled one side of the overalls and smiled as my look started coming together just perfectly.

"It did not," I replied. "But I appreciate the dig. Duly noted."

"Look, we all know about the famous RBJ time. My brother will have to learn this as well if he intends to spend a ton of time with you."

"You're not wrong, but I am going to *try* to be on time today. It's a rare, beautiful almost spring day in London, with just a little chill factor, so I want to take advantage of that… In the meantime, how does this look?"

As I walked from the mirror back to my laptop, I also started unpinning my hair so that my blond curls would have time to fall and create a sort of wavy, feathered look along the sides of my face. Facing the camera, I posed before Liv, letting her see multiple angles of me in the outfit.

"Okay, I sit corrected," she said. "Now I understand why you needed that top. You look absolutely gorgeous, Rob. Seriously."

"Thanks, Liv."

My cheeks flushed just slightly before I remembered all that I still had to do before I left—my makeup being tops on the list. And maybe seeing if I could get a little more intel on Craig from Liv.

"Now can we go back to this therapy thing? Why do you think Craig would hate you telling me?"

"Well, it's not that he's embarrassed of it, but I think a lot of people are not as open as you are when it comes to therapy. Day one, you were talking to me about finding a therapist in London, and I just don't know if he's there yet."

"You know what's funny? I wasn't always that way, but I figured that once I started it, the best way to not internalize it as something taboo was for me to casually talk about it in the same way I talk about getting a massage or buying a pair of shoes," I said with a shrug. "But I get it. Ironically, it makes me want to date him more knowing that he sees someone, so he shouldn't be ashamed of it at all. And I've actually been thinking about asking guys up front how they feel about it, especially since I have this vision of creating a perfect little therapy- and church-based family, where my husband has a person, I have a person and so do the kids."

"Is it complete with a white picket fence, too?"

"No, that would be too bland for me. But magenta? I'm not ruling it out!"

We laughed together as I picked up the laptop to bring it with me into the bathroom, where all my makeup products were and the lighting was better for applying liquid foundation and my fave Fenty bronzer.

"I want to ask more questions," I said as I sat down in the vanity chair I'd purchased after realizing that, yes, UK flats typically came with furniture, but there were specific items I needed personalized to fit my needs. My gold, silver and white vanity stool with a small back to it was one of those items. "But I also kind of feel like I'm peeking into Craig's diary, so maybe I should stop."

"If it makes you feel any better, I told him things about you, too."

"Oh my God, like what?"

"Mostly that you're amazing, you deserve the best

and I'll cut him if he hurts you. But Craig already knew all those things—especially the last part."

I looked at Liv through my bathroom mirror and smiled as I began applying my makeup.

"You're a good friend, Olivia."

"Only because you've been such a great one to me. I know part of the reason your bedroom looks like it does now—no shade, just saying—is because Frank and I have had you working long hours while we finalize this project."

"All the shade taken," I jokingly shouted back, trying not to laugh too hard as I meticulously traced the bottom of my eyes with a blue eyeliner that gave them just a tiny hint of an edge. Craig wasn't likely to notice, but I always felt like a badass when I wore this color, so it was really for me more than for him.

"And don't worry about my long hours. I love the work that you and Frank are doing, and I think it's going to pay off big-time. I can't wait to get the numbers back from him. If those are what I think they'll be, it'll all be worth it—then my room can go back to its immaculately presented normal self. And you'll be the next rock star of our company."

"Well, can this future rock star tell you one more thing?"

"Of course, anything."

"It's 2:45 p.m."

"Damn it!"

So much for my intentions of showing up on time. I needed at least five more minutes to finish my makeup, plus time to rake my hands through my hair for the final touch to my curls and a couple more minutes to brush my teeth, put on my shoes and say some affirming words. Then I still had at least a thirty-minute walk to the park. And all this needed to be done by three thirty. To say I was cutting it close was an understatement.

"Okay, let me go so I can try to get out of here in the next fifteen minutes."

"You got this. I believe in you."

"That might make one of us, but thank you!"

I hung up the call with Liv after a few goodbyes and genuine well-wishes from her, swiping my bronzer across my cheeks to achieve a sun-kissed look that was sparkly but also subtly made it seem like my skin was made to be on a beach somewhere.

"Today's going to be a great day," I said to myself.

As I stood up to run my hands through my hair, I caught glimpses of the slivers of skin showing at my waist through the side of my overalls—perfect for just a touch of sexiness—and happily noticed my blond curls starting to sculpt my face effortlessly. More than that, though, was the hint of a return to the superconfident version of me. For a final touch, I pulled out my bold red Ruby Woo lipstick and used it to color in my pouty lips. It was the denouement to my entire look and the perfect thing to encapsulate the feeling I had—that despite my nerves, things might finally be turning around.

Three minutes before 3:30 p.m., I sauntered into the southeast corner of Hyde Park on a mission to get to the Diana Huntress fountain, tucked in the Rose Garden, on time. Craig had chosen the location for us to meet ahead of time, noting that the Huntress fountain was the perfect landmark, since it was close to the entrance that I'd naturally walk into coming from my flat, and the area it took up was small enough that we'd quickly and easily spot each other. He also guaranteed that I'd love the beautiful beds of colorful roses in the garden, the herbal plants that complemented them and created this decadent smell you couldn't get out of your mind, and the peaceful quiet this part of the park afforded patrons—especially in areas like the benches under the pergola.

As I walked up to our meeting spot, enjoying the scenery almost as much as he'd predicted, I looked to my left and right to see if Craig had arrived yet. He had not. *Wouldn't it be ironic*, I thought, *if the one time I'm on time, the other person is late?* I didn't have long to contemplate my question, however, because I soon saw him in the distance, striding toward me like a scene out of a movie, somehow in slow motion while everything around him got hazy and he became the main focus in the frame. He wore a crisp gray T-shirt that looked as if it had been tailored perfectly, distressed jeans that stopped right above his ankles and the same gold chain he'd had on when we first met, plus the thousand-watt smile that had a hold on me in my dreams. And in his hands were a wicker picnic basket, and, amazingly, two long-stemmed peach camellia flowers. Olivia had obviously told him at least one more thing about me than she'd admitted to.

"Hi, there," he said softly as he drew closer to me.
"Hi."

Craig's smile never wavered, even as he stepped right into my space, setting the basket and flowers down. With a quick motion, he swiftly grabbed my arms and pulled me into a tight and warm embrace that we both lingered in for seconds, breathing deeply into the other's chest. His hands lightly dragged their way down my back until they reached their final destination at the top curve of my butt, wherein he firmly drew my body even more into his, using the opening of my overalls as his entry point. It was as if we were magnets, destined to be stuck to each other unless someone pulled us apart.

I lifted my head slightly so that my face was conveniently placed near his neck, getting a whiff of his cologne and allowing my breath to tickle his skin. In response, Craig shivered faintly and tilted his head down so that his lips hovered right above my nose.

"I guess I was really excited to see you again," he said, his voice cracking and coming out barely louder than a whisper. "A week feels like maybe too long? Good thing we're in public."

"That doesn't seem to be stopping us right now," I said, giggling into his chest.

"Trust me, I'm stopping myself from a lot right now."

After a few more seconds, we pulled out of the embrace, and I found myself surprisingly missing his touch already. *Calm down, Rob*, I admonished myself. *You can be excited to see him and keep your head about you.* And that was just what I planned to do, even as I caught Craig dragging his eyes over my body, pausing in just the places I'd envisioned when I chose the outfit.

"You brought flowers to a rose garden," I said as Craig picked his items back up, handed me the camellias and began leading me to one of the benches flanking the fountain. "Bold choice."

"Well, a little birdie told me these were your favorites. Plus, it's not like we can pick the roses, and I wanted you to have something to take home at the end of our date."

"Besides you," I asked jokingly.

Craig squinted at me and dipped his head into the nook of my neck without hesitation.

"Do you want the good guy, Robin?" he whispered. "Or the bad boy?"

"Can't I have both?"

I turned my head toward his—he was still breathing heavily into my neck—dropped my eyes and caught his before returning a playful smirk in his direction.

"You can have whatever you want," he said and then placed one soft, quick kiss on my neck before backing up.

"Do you know what you want?" he asked as a follow-up.

"I always think I do, but when it comes to relationships, I am generally proven wrong," I admitted.

I took my seat on one of the benches, and Craig followed suit, sitting diagonally across from me but allowing our knees to touch just slightly. Outwardly

I kept my composure, even as I was slowly freaking out in my head, wondering how he would react to me pivoting the conversation to something more vulnerable than sex—intimacy and fears. Craig didn't know it, but I'd actually considered the question he asked me quite often lately, so given the opportunity, I wanted to at least try to take it and be honest with him. Ultimately, I'd realized, that was definitely something I wanted: an honest and fun relationship that was just as comfortable in the sexy moments as it was in the vulnerable ones—and could slide back and forth between the two seamlessly.

I quietly held my breath as I waited for his response.

"I get that," he said, leaning his shoulder away from the bench so that he was almost acting as my protector on it, blocking me from any potential intruder while we spoke. "But if I could say yes and give you anything you wanted right now, what would that be?"

"Honestly, I'd just really like to get to know more about you," I said. "Beyond what your sister has already told me, of course."

"Of course," he said, rolling his eyes.

"You can't do that. Clearly, she told you things about me, too," I said, waving my flowers in the air.

"Yeah, but she told me good things about you. I'm sure all mine were bad."

"They weren't all bad."

I laughed and instinctively moved my hand to his thigh—a touch that was less brimming with sex and more of a reassurance that I was here because I wanted to be, no matter what he was worried she'd told me.

"I'm serious, though! Like, sure, I know you're a photographer and her baby brother, but what else? What is it that other people don't know?"

"Okay, deal. Can I get you to agree to the same?" he asked, holding out his pinkie finger to link it with mine and seal our pact.

"I'm an open book," I replied in protest.

"Hmm, not really."

Craig smacked his lips together and gave me a disbelieving look.

"Don't get me wrong—your whole boss-lady vibe is quite intriguing, but everyone knows that about you already. I want you to tell me what keeps you up at night, what genuinely makes you laugh, what makes you squirm in good and bad ways, and all the other stuff you hold back because you don't feel safe enough to share it."

"We've known each other a week and you want me to share all my deep, dark secrets?"

"Yeah," he replied, still holding his hand in the air and daring me to take it.

"But how do I know I can trust you? I have some of the best friends in the world, and they don't know everything about me."

"I know," he said matter-of-factly. "And you don't know—that's why it's called trust."

Craig tilted his head to the side, showing me the pearly whites of his eyes as he patiently waited for me to say yes. I stared back, excited about his proposal and equally scared at the thought of letting my guard down with him just to be hurt again. Robin, meet stove once again, I thought, hoping I wouldn't get burned this time. Here was this man asking me to trust him when he hadn't done anything yet to earn it, and yet even with my fear lingering, I couldn't shake the thought that I would regret not at least trying.

I mean, he was saying exactly what I wanted him to say, so why did it feel like my chest was caving in?

With a quick sigh, I forced my hand up and locked pinkies with him before I could talk myself out of it—praying the entire time I wasn't setting myself up for failure.

"Deal," I responded and watched his lips curl into a smile that lit up his face. "So where do we start?"

"Well, I can tell you more about my photography and what I love about it. Or did Liv break that down for you already?"

"She didn't," I said, sitting up and positioning my chest slightly closer to him as I readied myself for my first set of *all mine* details from Craig.

"Good. Okay, so I started taking photos about a decade ago, just walking around Brixton, trying to see my surroundings from a different vantage point," he said. "You know, I'd grown up there all my life, but I knew I wasn't seeing it for all that it was. I guess it's easy to take things for granted when it's just there."

"I know that feeling. I lived in DC for so long, and it took me an embarrassingly long time before I visited all the monuments and stuff there. Once I did, I was so upset with myself for just ignoring these beautiful structures practically in my backyard when people paid hundreds of dollars to travel to DC so they could see them in person."

"Exactly. Brixton has all these beautiful parks and murals, and I just walked past them all my life, never taking moments to appreciate them. I was also a stubborn lad—just twenty years old—and trying to figure out what I wanted to do with my life. I knew I didn't want to be corporate like you and my sister—you know, she was already starting to climb that ladder, and I just had no desire. So, I leaned into this photography thing. And it was kinda like Darius in *Love Jones*, really. I found my love for it when I noticed my eye was drawn to capturing how the people interacted with each other and all the bits around them."

I scrunched my face at Craig's *Love Jones* reference, looking at him quizzically as I contemplated whether I wanted to interrupt the great story he was telling with a fact check. There he was, breaking down for me all the details of how he'd come to be a photographer—one whose lifestyle portraits ultimately ended up in magazines like British *GQ* and *Porter*. It was amazing, and I wanted to know more, but I wasn't going to be able to focus with him making such a glaring error about one of the most iconic Black American movies of all time.

"Um, I'm sorry? Who did you say was the photographer in *Love Jones*?" I asked, unable to hold in my question any longer.

"Darius," he answered quickly but then questioned himself. "Right?"

"Absolutely not! How does someone who does this

for a living not remember that Nina was the photographer? It was, like, a major part of her storyline."

I squinched my eyes at Craig again and watched his face for recognition. He was completely clueless, I realized. And then it dawned on me...

"Oh!" I screamed out. "You haven't ever seen it. Have you?"

"Well..."

"Tell the truth."

"I've seen bits and pieces!"

I took in a huge, shocked breath and dropped my mouth in disbelief, holding back the laughter that wanted to pour out of me.

"How is this possible?" I asked. "You, the man who convinced me that he was a romcom fanatic despite my initial misgivings, have not only never seen it, you're walking around perpetrating like you have!"

"I know all the important parts."

"But obviously you don't, if you thought that Darius was the photographer! How do you explain his poem, 'A Blues for Nina,' if he's not the poet, Craig?"

He started to speak and then I stopped him again.

"Wait, you do know about the 'A Blues for Nina' poem, right?"

"Of course I do," he said in his defense while I looked upon him with my mouth wide-open, amazed at the audacity. "That's up there with the 'just as you are' scene in *Bridget Jones's Diary*. What Black man hasn't asked 'is that all right?' in Darius's signature singsongy inflection as a cheat-code way to seduce a woman?"

"I don't know! Maybe the same man who's never seen the movie."

"I'm never living this down, am I?"

"You definitely are not. Like, why bring it up if you haven't seen it?! You know what? Never mind. We just need to go ahead and make a date for you to watch it at my place one night, because this has to be rectified ASAP. I can't have you walking around like this. Does your sister know about this abomination?"

"I'm not sure if she's seen it, either, to be honest."

"What?!"

"I see that this is very important to you," he said, laughing at my continued amazement.

"Yeah, I don't think you understand," I said, shaking my head. "Maybe it wasn't the same for people here. But in America, *Love Jones* was the first time a lot of us saw beautiful young Black people on the big screen, falling in love and not in some sort of downtrodden life struggle at the same time. They weren't rich, but they were comfortable, and their friends seemed real and funny and complicated, and the chemistry between Nia Long and Larenz Tate was just out of this world. Top that off with the fact that it was shot in Chicago—my hometown—like, it's just one of those movies that is indelible to my life story."

"Wow, okay, now, see? When you talk about it like that, it makes me want to see it."

I put my head in my hands and laughed to myself.

"You would also love it because of the cinematography, I think. The way they shot it, how their brown skin glows in the camera—it's beautiful to watch, too. And don't get me wrong—in current eyes, there's definitely lots of toxicity in the relationships that are shown. But man, the heat factor alone, plus all the quotables? I just can't believe you haven't seen it!"

"I know, but we're fixing that, so it'll be fine."

"Yes, we are. And soon."

"I like soon," Craig said, smiling back at me. "I get no credit for at least knowing some parts of it, though?"

"Okay, you can get *some* credit if you can tell me what Darius makes for Nina after the first night they spend together."

"Pancakes?"

"Aw, naw," I said, throwing my hands in the air. "You get none. No credit whatsoever… It was an omelet. He got up and made her an omelet while wearing just a pair of jeans. And I decided then that if a man ever did the same, I'd marry him."

Craig raised his eyebrows at me and flashed a curious look my way.

"I'm obviously still single," I replied, responding to his nonverbal question.

"Duly noted, as you say. That would seem like an easy request to fulfill, though, no?"

"Well, I'd never told any man I was dating until just now," I admitted. "You know, I'm trying out this whole trust thing, right?"

"It looks good on you," he said with a smile and then looked at our surroundings. "Okay, let's leave these benches and find ourselves a spot in the grass where we can eat properly and you can tell me more of the secret tests you have for your future husband."

"Not tests, but sure. I was enjoying learning about you, too, though. I just couldn't let you keep going with that horrible Darius take."

"No, I appreciate it. Especially because I learned some valuable intel, anyway."

Craig took my hand in his as we stood up from the benches and began walking down the curved path of the pergola to get to our next destination. Passing the Holocaust and Queen Caroline memorials, we finally stopped just at the edge of the Serpentine Lake, where the park opened up to the greenest of grass and you could sit down with a view of the water and many of the other park attractions in clear view. There, we found our own little patch of land to take over, and Craig started laying out the blanket he'd stuffed into the basket.

"You thought of everything," I said happily as I sat down on one side and watched him spread out containers of grapes, strawberries, cheese and meat before us. Lastly, he pulled out a bottle of sauvignon blanc and two cups.

"I like you, Robin," he said with a straight face, staring deeply into my eyes. "I know that you know a bit about my past, but I'm not interested in being the guy who plays games anymore. So, if it means putting in a little extra effort so that you believe that eventually, I'm going to do that."

An unstoppable smile grew on my face even as I tried to bite my lower lip to contain it.

"Okay," I said, gazing back into his eyes.

"Plus, it's not lost on me that I'm on a date with you

on the prince's home turf. I couldn't exactly come here empty-handed."

"Eric and I never came here, actually," I responded.

"Really?"

"Nope. That was part of the problem. We never went anywhere, because we didn't want the paparazzi to catch wind."

Eric opened the bottle of wine and began pouring some into our glasses as I unsealed the container of grapes and grabbed a handful of my own.

"How did you not feel like a secret?"

"I did. And like some sort of weird friend with benefits, even though we had all the other parts of a relationship happening. Like, my family knew about him. My friends met him, albeit briefly. He claimed that people knew about me, but we were never able to intertwine our lives together for real. So, ultimately, it just felt…"

"Fake."

"Yeah."

"And you want—"

"So much real. It's like you said earlier—I want all the dirty parts that people try to hide, that I try to hide, to be wide-open in my next relationship. I want to feel like there's nothing my partner can't tell me and there's no hidden agendas between us—we're just disgustingly honest with each other all the time."

"Thank you for finally answering my question from earlier," Craig said as he passed me my cup of wine. "You know exactly what you want."

"But I don't know how doable it is."

"I'm willing to see if you are."

Craig raised his cup in the air and waited for me to lift mine so that we could slap them together like two people getting ready to shout, "Cheers!" He didn't have to wait long, as I quickly joined him, without hesitation this time, but still a quiet prayer in my heart all the same.

Chapter Thirteen

As the sun began to set, producing this beautiful purplish-pink sky over the park, Craig and I finished the last drops that remained in our wine bottle and I sat marveling at the sights before me, secretly wishing we weren't about to call it a night any time soon. In the hour or so since we'd moved from the bench to the blanket and convened our late lunch, my attraction to him had only grown as we discussed everything from our favorite sports teams (Bulls for me, Lakers for him) and zodiac sign compatibility (Could an Aries woman and Leo man work? Guess we'd find out!) to dating deal breakers (for Craig, people who take themselves too seriously; for me, liars), all with that mixture of fun, steaminess and openness I'd been craving for so long.

"So, do you think you want to stay in London long term?" Craig asked as he finished packing up the now-empty containers and started to stretch out his legs on the blanket.

"Honestly, I don't know," I responded. "I could see myself here for at least a few years, though. The goal was certainly never to come and leave within a year, that's for sure."

"Because you have all these ambitious plans for how you want to make your mark in the investment world, right?"

"That, yes, but also, as much as I loved DC and I adore the people there, I just felt like I needed to make a change to break out of my comfort zone. By the time I was campaigning for my new job, I could basically do everything I was doing there with my eyes closed, you know? I went there for college and stayed, so all my friends—except one—have basically been the same for over a decade. I've had the same favorite places to go for years now, *and* it felt like I was dating the same guy over and over in a different body. I'd even gotten into a traveling routine, where I was just used to leaving for a few weeks at a time for work every four to six months, going back and then waiting for the next reason to take a trip."

"I could see how that would feel like you were in a rut," Craig said, laying his head down just inches away from my right thigh.

"Exactly. But here, I feel challenged at my job again, I'm forced to get to know new people, and I'm learning more about myself…so I wouldn't want to just pack up and leave all that anytime soon. But I haven't gotten as far as knowing whether I see myself here in ten years or something, or even five, for that matter."

"You? You don't have a ten-year plan?" Craig asked with his voice dripping in sarcasm. "I'm shocked."

"I know. I'm the ten-year-plan queen!"

"I know you are."

"But I didn't want to do that when I moved here."

"Good for you," he said, looking up at me from the blanket as I continued sitting crisscross-style with my legs underneath me. "I'm sure that was hard."

"It definitely has been. When you're used to knowing what you want far out in advance and planning your life around getting it, it's sort of a shock to the system to just stop cold turkey."

"What was the last big goal you set?"

"And achieved?"

"Either. Both."

"The last big one I set and accomplished was getting my promotion to move here. Then there were all these smaller ones related to that, like getting the flat I wanted, some of the furniture I wanted, etc."

"Mmm-hmm, okay. That makes sense."

"And the last one I set but haven't achieved yet…"

I grimaced, stopping myself before I could finish my sentence and wondering if I was ready to be this honest with Craig. It had the potential to completely scare him off, but I'd made a deal with him, so I wanted to follow through with it. Hopefully, he wouldn't get up and run as fast and as far away as he could, I thought.

I inhaled deeply and let the air escape from my lips as I spoke my next words.

"Was to be in a relationship before I turned thirty-one."

Craig lifted his head up so that he could search my face, and I waited with bated breath to see how he'd respond to that kind of confession on a first date. He didn't say a word but instead pursed his lips as he nodded in understanding, and then after a long beat, he burst into laughter, his head falling directly into my lap.

"How's that going so far?" he asked as he tried to catch his breath.

"Yeah, well, I think you know it wasn't going well. It was going really horribly, actually," I said, joining him in tears of laughter. "Until…"

"Until what?" Craig asked, his face suddenly turning serious as he locked eyes with me again.

I stared back, not knowing what to say, exactly. There was a part of me that was hoping to finish the sentence with "until I met you," but it felt too soon to say something like that, even if it was how I felt. Another part of me had given up on my whole plan anyway, ready to just surrender and settle into whatever timing God and the universe had for me. And still another part of me was defiant and refused to give up, ready to keep trying even if this experiment with us was a bust. I didn't know how to say all that without sounding like a blubbering mess or like he was just a means to an end, which he wasn't, so I simply shrugged my shoulders, pressed my lips together, and silently mouthed, *I don't know.*

Craig nodded his head again and rested it back on my lap, choosing not to press the matter this time around. For the next few minutes, I sat and he lay on the blanket in silence, neither of us knowing what to say next. It wasn't until I started to feel the pitter-patters of raindrops falling onto my skin that I finally found some words to say to him again.

"Is that rain?" I asked.

I raised my hand to my side to see if, somehow, I'd made it up, but no, there they were…little puddles of water forming in my hand.

"We should probably head out," Craig said, forcing himself up from the ground. "I don't want you to get caught in a bad storm going back home. The weather has a way of turning in an instant here."

As he stood up, I instantly felt an emptiness in the pit of my stomach from no longer feeling his touch, and while I was thankful the rain had broken our silence, I was keenly aware Craig hadn't looked in my direction since I'd lost my words earlier. I also knew that despite whatever awkwardness was happening, I wasn't ready for our time to end just yet.

"Do you want to come back to my place?" I asked, the words coming out of my mouth as a sort of gentle plea.

While I waited for him to answer, I stood up, too, and grabbed my end of the blanket to start folding it. Regardless of what we decided, it was clear we needed to start making our way out of the park before the little droplets turned into big plops of water and then a downpour.

"I mean, I don't know if you had other plans already," I added, offering him an out—even though I didn't want him to take it—as his silence continued. "But if not, you're welcome to stay for a bit."

Finally, as Craig stepped closer to me so that we could bring our two blanket ends together to finish the fold, he tilted his head down and met my insistent eyes.

"Are you sure?"

The tone in his voice seemed like that of a man still trying to figure me out, but also maybe not quite convinced it was worth it. Taking the last corner from my grasp, he placed the folded blanket in the basket and then handed me the flowers again while he waited for my confirmation.

"Yeah, of course," I replied, hoping to make myself clear where I hadn't before. "I wouldn't offer if I didn't mean it."

"Okay, then yeah, I'd like that."

Craig's lips curled into a crooked smile as I watched the light in his eyes flicker again.

"On one condition…"

"Uh-oh, what's that?"

"We make sure to watch *Love Jones* before I leave."

"That's the easiest thing I've agreed to all day!"

"I thought it might be," he said, his face now beaming with joy.

I playfully pushed his arm and rolled my eyes, giving Craig just the opportunity to grab my hand and take it in his.

"You better be happy I like you," he said.

"Oh, you like me?"

"That's not obvious to you by now?"

"Maybe a girl just needs to confirm sometimes."

"I'm down for as much confirmation as you need, Robin," Craig said, gripping my hand tighter in his. "But for now, we really need to go, because it looks like we might be in trouble.

As the rain started falling a little harder, the two of us began walking back into the direction of the Rose Garden and the park exit. Hand in hand, we watched as the gray sky grew darker, ominously looming over us and forcing us to pick up our speed so that, fifteen minutes into our journey, we were almost practically running in lockstep. It was equal parts funny and scary as we found ourselves stubbornly in a race with Mother Nature to see who would win out.

The problem was that while we were making good time, as we got closer to our destination, the rain seemed to come down harder than ever, pelting us with large drops of water and soaking our clothes. We were about two blocks away from my flat when we were officially defeated; the sky seemed to completely open up and gushes of rainwater poured down onto us. At that point all we could do was hold on tight to each other and keep going toward our proverbial light at the end of the tunnel—the green landmark of Vincent Square telling us we were almost home safe.

"Oh my God," I screamed as we ran into my lobby, every piece of us dripping wet from both rain and sweat. "That was insane!"

"I know," Craig said, shaking his head. "But we made it."

"Did we?" I raised my arm to show him just how drenched my clothes were and the sad state of my flowers, which had definitely seen better days.

"Well, when you put it like that, maybe we didn't."

Craig laughed as he attempted to squeeze some of the water out of his shirt before we walked farther into the lobby, inevitably leaving damp footsteps on our path to the elevator. When we stepped in, still holding hands, I caught myself watching his face to see if I could tell what he was thinking. It had only been a week since I'd made a similar trek with Zayn, and I wasn't exactly in the mood to be blindsided at my front door again.

Craig's brow furrowed into a puzzled expression as we watched the numbers on the elevator climb to my floor. Finally, as the doors opened and we walked out, he turned to me and spoke.

"Robin," he said, shaking his head again.

I looked back at him, trying not to jump to conclusions and choosing to remain calm while he finished his statement.

"Why didn't we just hail a black cab?"

"Oh my God," I responded. "Why *didn't* we hail a cab?! What were we thinking?"

Tears of laughter formed as I realized how ridiculous it was that we'd chosen to run back thirty minutes in the rain. That decision had to have been courtesy of the bottle of wine we'd drunk; there was no other way around it.

"I don't know, but whatever the reason, I'm blaming it on you. Just so you know."

"On me?! You're the one who's lived here all twenty-nine years of his life."

"No, no, length of stay doesn't count here," he joked. "We were coming back to your place, and it was a walk you'd already made, so you had to have known our chances of getting back here dry were slim."

Craig gripped my hand tightly as we walked to my front door, making sure not to let me out of his grasp even as we took playful digs at each other.

"I guess maybe I was a little too distracted to make that kind of a rational decision," I admitted as I turned the key in the lock. "But that still brings the blame back to you. You're the distracting one!"

"If that's the rationale, then we both take the blame."

"Fine," I said, rolling my eyes.

With a small push of my door, Craig and I walked into the foyer, immediately sliding off our wet sneakers and peeling off the first layer of our clothes.

"Let me go get you some towels," I said, reluctantly letting go of his hand and walking toward the bathroom. "We can throw these clothes in the tumbler real quick, but I should also have some oversize items you can put on in the meantime."

Stepping into the bathroom, I grabbed two large towels and my white cotton-terry robe. Then I ran to my room to try to straighten up a little and look for an oversize T-shirt and basketball shorts that might fit Craig's six-foot, muscular body. This might have been the one time it worked in my favor that I was five-nine myself with thick thighs, so I thought I might be in luck. It took me a little more than four to five minutes all told, but soon I was walking back to my foyer to present Craig with a litany of items to help him feel more comfortable.

When I turned the corner, I was the one greeted with a surprise, however, as his deep brown skin flashed before me—showing everywhere, from his chest to his calves.

"Oh," I managed to mutter out under my breath.

I closed my mouth in an attempt to swallow down my shock of seeing him standing there in nothing but a pair of charcoal-gray boxer briefs.

"Sorry." He shrugged sheepishly. "I was just getting really cold standing in those damp clothes."

"No, it's fine," I said blinking myself back into reality so that I could once again move my limbs.

One step at a time, I walked closer to Craig until I was near enough to see the goose bumps forming in the little hairs on his chest. I knew enough not to let my eyes drag down any farther if I wanted us to make it past the foyer, so with deep concentration, I handed him one of the towels and fought the electricity that soared through my spine as our fingertips lightly touched during the exchange.

"I also…um…have some clothes you may be able to fit into," I said, shoving those toward him as well.

"Thank you."

"No problem," I responded, suddenly needing to leave his presence as fast as I could before I gave in to the images flashing before my eyes—of our wet bodies crashing into my hallway walls while we sucked on each other's lips, necks and beyond. I swallowed hard and pivoted away from him to head back to my room.

"I'll be right back," I said, trying not to look his way so that I wouldn't be caught in the vortex of his achingly enticing eyes again.

"Okay."

Craig reached out his hand and grabbed mine before I could leave, forcing me to turn back to him and look into his face.

"Yes?"

"Nothing. I just needed to touch you again."

"Um, you can go in the living room when you're done," I said, totally unable to even think of a response to what he'd just admitted out loud. "I'll get your clothes and put them in the dryer when I get back."

I dropped my eyes in a hurry and practically ran back to my room. Once in there, I toweled down my hair, squeezed myself out of my wet overalls and replaced the black lace bra and panties I'd been wearing with a new nude pair that almost perfectly matched the color of my brown skin. Then I slid on my robe, tied it tightly around my waist and took in a deep sigh before scooping up my pile of wet items to bring with me to the kitchen. As I passed by the living room, I saw Craig sitting on my couch, his legs spread wide, wearing my white T-shirt and blue shorts that fit him almost the same as the boxer briefs.

"So, the shorts didn't exactly work out," I said as I quickly sauntered by so that I could get his clothes from the hallway and add them to my pile.

"Yeah, my legs seem to be quite a bit bigger than yours. But they'll do," he shouted back.

Visions of his wanton thighs flickered before me at the thought. Clearly, he was right. And as I recalled how he'd stood fully exposed in my hallway, I remembered that there was something else down there that was quite a bit bigger than I'd assumed as well.

"Pull yourself together," I mumbled under my breath as I threw our clothes into the dryer and set the timer.

"What was that?" he asked from the couch.

"Nothing!" I responded and then mumbled again, "Just over here talking to myself like a crazy person."

Once I heard the dryer turn on, I finally made my way to my living room to join Craig on the couch. He was still waiting in that same addictive position when I walked in and plonked myself next to him.

"Cute robe," he said, kneading the hem of it that fell to just about midthigh.

"Ha-ha, thank you."

I dared to look him in his eyes again as I repositioned myself so that I was sitting sideways on the couch, my body fully facing his.

"So, now that we're both dry, what do you want to do?" I asked.

"If you're completely dry," he responded, dropping his eyes and purposely letting them linger on my breasts and then on my thighs, where my robe slightly opened before him, "I'm not exactly doing my job right."

"Craig!"

"Just saying." He shrugged.

"Well, maybe not completely dry," I said, smiling mischievously and biting my lower lip.

"Hmm."

Craig scootched himself slightly closer to me, so that his thigh was directly touching my knees, and I felt the all-too-familiar tingles of absolute, unmistakable desire flush over me.

"Anyway, I know a lot has happened since we were talking about this, but I do want to go back to our conversation about ten-year plans and ruts."

"Really?" he asked with a smirk.

"Yes, really. Indulge me here, please."

"Okay, you got it," he said, lifting his eyes back to mine. "Let's talk about plans and ruts."

"Well, you know where I stand with them right now. What about you?"

"Mmm."

Craig sat back on the couch and thought. After a few moments, he looked my way again so that he could respond.

"Honestly, I've never really been a long-term-plan kinda guy. I have goals, obviously, but I picked a profession that affords me with a lot of flexibility on purpose."

"Yeah."

"I also don't get in a lot of ruts, per se, because of that. The beauty of being a photographer is that the nature of what I do is always changing. I might take an assignment in Scotland tomorrow and then Nigeria the next week and then decide to stay home for a while so

I can capture some of the raw images of the London you probably don't see on your TV back in America."

"It sounds exciting," I said, leaning my side into the couch just a little closer to his frame.

"It is, yeah."

"Is your lifestyle also why you haven't really wanted a relationship before?"

"Eh, some of it. I'm not going to lie to you—there can be a lot of wild nights out there if I want to engage in that. And I've had my fair share of doing so, getting caught in lies with the women I was dating, all because I wanted to be able to have fun but also have access to them whenever I was home, even though I knew they wanted more."

I shuddered a little listening to him speak. It was great that he was being so honest, but damn, his words seemed to trigger a raw nerve I thought had healed by now.

"So, why not just be honest with them?" I asked. "Maybe they would have agreed to your terms, but instead, you lied. That's…"

"I know. Unforgivable."

Craig turned his head to face me, and I felt myself soften under his gaze. His words were upsetting, sure, but as I watched and listened to him, they sounded more like those coming from a contrite man than someone making excuses to continue leading the same life.

"The thing is, I understand now that part of why I was doing all that was because I didn't believe the women I was dating would want me for me. I thought I had to lie to them, because who would take me as I am—handsome, yes—" He paused before continuing, his lips curling into a smile. "But flawed AF."

Leaning his head back, Craig rested it on the back cushions and positioned himself so that his nose was almost touching mine.

"And, Robin, the thing you should know is, I don't have a desire to change my career and the lifestyle that comes with it. A lot of women are not going to like that, but it's true. That part hasn't changed for me. Now... I just... I want to be able to spend it honestly with some-one along for the ride."

Craig dropped his eyes down to my lips and breathed on them slightly.

"Is that all right?" he asked with a smirk, invoking Larenz Tate's iconic singsongy tone.

I bit my lip, fighting to hold back my giggles and the toe-curling feeling I had watching him stare at my mouth.

"Robin," Craig said, still not moving his eyes. "I know I'm kinda joking, but I'm also being as honest with you as I know how, so I do need to know if that's something you'd be okay with."

"As long as you keep being this straightforward with me," I replied, "I'm here."

In response, Craig quickly lifted his eyes toward mine, and I could see the happiness in them. And sud-denly, I wasn't sure if it was the look in his eyes or the ever-growing tingling feeling in my vagina, but I could no longer resist how much I wanted him.

"Craig," I asked, drawing myself even closer to him. "Do you want to kiss me?"

"What kind of question is that?"

"A genuine one."

He shifted in his seat and repositioned himself so that we were fully facing each other.

"Do you remember earlier today when I said I was stopping myself?"

"Yes."

"I've been stopping myself since the first time I laid eyes on you."

"From kissing me?"

"From doing every filthy thing imaginable with you...starting with kissing...and licking...and biting... every inch of your body."

As Craig slowly listed just some of the things that he wanted to do to me, my insides pulsed with a fervor I could no longer contain. And before I knew it, I'd leaned into him, pressing my lips firmly into his, in search of his tongue, with all my inhibitions thrown fully to the side. Seizing his opportunity, Craig quickly wrapped his arms around me and pulled my torso in closer so that our chests were literally heaving on each other as the ache we'd both felt was released into a deep, long, passionate kiss. His right hand then slid up my back until he grabbed a handful of my damp curls and, pulling my neck open to him, Craig dived his mouth into the nook right above my collarbone and traced light circles with his tongue before replacing them with small nibbles.

Fueled by his assertiveness, I lifted my left thigh and straddled Craig's lap—instantly feeling the electricity and heat between us as our private parts connected. The flimsy bit of coverage provided by my underwear and the shorts that fit him like boxer briefs was certainly not enough to prevent him from feeling how drenched I was as I sat down onto his covered but still very rock-hard penis. And it only served to ignite even more the fire that was burning inside us.

I lifted Craig's head from my neck, needing to feel his mouth on mine again, and pressed deeply as our tongues intertwined and our lips engaged in the most sensual and pleasurable dance.

Eventually, Craig shifted his legs underneath me and flipped us both so that my back was on the couch and his body was draped on top of mine. From there, he lightly dragged his tongue across my chin, down my throat, then to the top of my chest, where he lingered just slightly at the opening of my robe before skipping down to the bottom of my robe. At my legs, he began placing small bites all around the inner parts of my left thigh and then my right, giving them equal, mind-blowing attention.

"Oh my God," I moaned, losing all control of my body and readily giving it over to him to do what he liked.

Craig must have sensed this, as he lifted his eyes in response, locked his with mine and smiled deviously.

"I can stop now if you want. I believe we were supposed to be watching *Love Jones*, right?"

"Screw *Love Jones*," I said, throwing my head back. "All I want right now is you."

That was all Craig needed to hear as he quickly untied my robe, opening it to expose my body before him, and slid my panties down the sides of my legs. Without another word, he looked at me once more, licked his lips and buried his head into the folds of the vagina that had been calling out to him all day.

Now, it was all his to do with as he pleased.

He knew it, and I knew it, too.

Chapter Fourteen

The familiar tip-taps of keyboard typing from the early birds in our building greeted me as I stepped onto the floor designated for our marketing and portfolio teams. On the marketing side of the suite, I passed about three people already in their cubicles, plugging away as they guzzled down whatever their chosen poison was between coffee and tea. I had a feeling it was going to be at least three cups for me, mostly because close to four weeks into us dating, Craig and I were still pulling all-nighters, either in person or on the phone like a couple of high school kids sprung on each other. And yet, as much I enjoyed the time we spent together, it didn't change the fact that I needed to get to work every weekday by 8:30 a.m.

This was especially no easy feat this morning, as

Craig had taken particular pleasure in torturing me with flirty texts even as I tried to get ready. Thankfully, I'd made the smart decision to pick out and iron my outfit the night before—a dark mustard blazer and matching tank top with a pair of flared, wide-leg, burnt orange dress pants—so all I had to do when I got up was shower and brush my teeth, unwrap my hair, put on some makeup, and slip on what I'd already chosen. And since I was meeting him once again after work, I also threw in my work bag all the items I needed to switch my corporateish outfit into something more appropriate for a nightclub, including a pair of high-waisted, ripped wide-leg jeans and some chunky, clear heels.

Now, I just had to get through the day without dozing off, something that I hoped would be made easier by what I was expecting to be a good report from Frank on his and Olivia's latest investment fund portfolio. I made my way to my office with my phone still in hand as I continued responding to texts from the man who was still in his bed and didn't need to be anywhere for at least another hour.

Craig: I hope you're ready for tonight. I'm excited to finally show you just a taste of Brixton.

Oh, I'm very ready, or I will be once I get some coffee in me.

Craig: Were you up late or something?

I could hear his mischievous grin through our texts; *what had I gotten myself into?* I thought. Who thought it was a good idea to start falling for a captivatingly delicious man who had the playful nature of a child?

Yes, I think so, I replied. Some beautiful British man just wouldn't stop talking to me.

Craig: Wow. Well, I can't imagine what he'll do tonight when you're in his arms, slow grinding to African and Caribbean beats under the dim lights of the club. You might have to watch out for his tongue dipping into all the exposed parts of your skin. *tongue emoji*

Good thing for me there won't be much exposed, I responded, typing with a huge grin plastered on my face as I walked into my office.

Craig: Wait, you're not wearing your work clothes tonight, right?

Please. Have more faith in me than that. You happen to be dating the master of transitioning from work wear to club attire.

Craig: Then I'm not worried, because I'm a master of finding the exposed parts. Plus, regardless of whatever frock you're wearing, my goal is for it to be in a pile on the floor in my flat by the end of the night.

OMG, Craig. I'm at work lol

Craig: Sorry, I just haven't been able to stop thinking about how those perky nipples of yours feel on my tongue. And I want it again.

Okay, if I didn't stop him now, I realized, I was going to be caught squirming at my desk in my very glass office.

I know what you're doing, you scoundrel, and it's not going to work lol. I'm going now before I have to go to the bathroom and dry off my underwear before I've even checked my emails.

Craig: Okay, okay. I'll let you go. But tonight, you're all mine. Oh, and tell my sis I said hello.

No no no, you can't bring up your sister right after you mention wanting to use your mouth on various parts of my body!

Craig: It's called balance, babe. You'll be okay lol. Now, go, before I say more of what I want to do to you in that fancy little glass office of yours. I'm trying to be good.

Ugh, bye. You're the worst.

Craig: You love it. *wink emoji*

I barely had time to let his last statement ruminate in my head before Frank and Olivia walked in, their faces lit up with joy. I quickly made sure my phone was silenced and turned the screen over before giving them my full attention. The last thing I needed was Olivia—or Frank, for that matter—seeing any sort of naughty notification come through from Craig while we were talking business, and I didn't quite trust that he wouldn't send one at the least appropriate time.

"Oh hi, guys! Come on in. You look happy."

The two of them practically skipped into my office and sat down in the two chairs facing my desk, looking at each other with wide smiles as they did.

"We have some amazing news," Frank said.

"Yeah, like knock-your-socks-off, make-your-whole-day, maybe even make-your-whole-week type of news," chimed in Olivia.

"Okay, the suspense is killing me. Spill the beans, please."

Frank turned his head from Olivia's and looked at me, then squinted his eyes and furrowed his brow.

"I don't know, Olivia. She seems pretty happy already, right? Like, maybe even glowy?"

"She does seem glowy. Could this have anything to do with a certain someone?" Olivia asked.

"Um, I thought you all were coming in here to tell *me* something, not give me the third degree," I responded, feeling my skin blush from within.

"Okay, okay, we'll stop torturing you," said Olivia.

"Please do."

"Because even if it's in addition to whatever's got you grinning like it's your birthday, it's a damn good addition," added Frank.

"OMG. Tell me!"

The two looked at each other again, and Olivia squealed as Frank broke the news.

"So, you know how we all had a feeling this portfolio was going to be a success…"

"Yes?"

"It's better than we could have imagined. We just found out that we got 130 percent of the investors we were expecting, and we exceeded our fund-raising goal by 115 percent, and—"

"We raised $500 million!" Olivia added, interrupting Frank's spiel before quickly turning to him with an apology. "Sorry, I couldn't hold it in."

"This is fantastic news," I shouted, rising in my seat. "You two should be so proud of your work."

"It's definitely a team effort," Olivia remarked. "We couldn't have done this without your support."

"Yeah, but I wouldn't have had anything to support if the two of you didn't push for trying something different this time around. I love it. This makes all those long nights worth it, right?"

"So worth it," they repeated in unison.

"Okay, so we definitely have to celebrate. I'm talking far more than Nando's today for lunch, so think about where you want to go and I'll make it happen. But also, I'd love it, Frank, if you could put together a presentation that talks about lessons learned from this and where you think we can go even further with our marketing ideas now. Olivia, obviously, I know your team has plenty of other things to worry about, but it would be great if you could put your eyes on that before Frank's done so that we're sure to have your input, too."

"Of course, I'll make the time," she said, looking back and forth between me and Frank. "That's not a problem at all."

"Great, because, Frank, really, I see this serving as such a great model for what our team does going forward. I think we knew instinctively that tailoring the messaging to reach the millennial audience through digital campaigns was the right way to go, but it's so nice to have the evidence to back it up it now. Do you have anything that shows what was most impactful to the campaign?"

"Well, funny enough, I thought it was going to be the videos, but it turns out it seems to have been a combination of the dynamic website that allowed users to interact with the different parts of the portfolio to determine what works best for them—and, get this, the photos. I definitely have Olivia to thank for that last part."

"Oh?"

I looked in Liv's direction, my face inadvertently scrunching up before I could stop it.

"Did Craig have something to do with the portfolio?" I asked.

"Yeah," she said, hesitating a bit. "Did he not tell you? He consulted with us from the very beginning and took all the photos for the campaign."

"Oh…uh, no, he didn't say anything."

I sat back in my seat, trying to hold back my shock and a little bit of disappointment. It wasn't that I was upset that Craig had worked on this project with my and Olivia's team—far from it. I knew by now how great he was at his job. But it was the fact that he hadn't been the one to tell me that produced that pit-in-the-stomach feeling I'd managed to avoid with him so far.

Despite my best attempts to keep my cool, Olivia must have seen my reaction, because she immediately tried to speak up in his defense.

"He probably just thought I'd already told you or something," she said, her face slightly cringing off to the side of Frank.

"Oh wait, is Olivia's brother the reason you were lit up like a Christmas tree when we walked in?" Frank asked, bobbing his head between us two as realization swept over him.

"We've been dating for a few weeks now."

I tried repositioning myself in my chair so that I wouldn't look so pathetic in front of my friends, who just so happened to also be my employee and my colleague. We all had a pretty casual working relationship, considering Frank and I had come up in the company together and Olivia and I had gone out for drinks two days after meeting each other, but still, finding out something I didn't know about the guy I liked in a business meeting wasn't exactly the boss-lady image I prided myself on portraying.

"Well, first, he's scrumptious, so good for you, Robin," Frank said, nodding in approval. "But second, you tell him I said if he's going to work with us in the future—and I really hope he is, he's amazing—he can't make the boss mad by not telling her."

Leave it to Frank to break up the tension in the room. We all cracked up laughing, and I settled back in my seat, thankful to have people around me I could count on to do good work and make a great joke at the perfect time.

"I'll be sure to convey that message," I said with a giggle.

Thank you, Olivia mouthed to Frank and then turned her attention back to me. "All right, the work never stops, so I have to get back to portfolio land. We just had to come and tell you this good news as soon as we got it."

She stood and Frank quickly followed, both of them pep stepping their way back to my door.

"Thanks guys, I appreciate it. And again, I'm so very happy for you. You did it!"

"We did it," Frank said, giving me my patented wink as he walked out the door.

As soon as they were gone, I turned my phone back over, and as I expected, saw I'd missed a text from Craig. It was a picture of him smiling with his camera swung around his arm and a caption:

No need to respond. Just wanted you to know that you're not the only one heading to work with thoughts swirling of the two of us.

What I mean to say is, I can't stop thinking about you, Robin. And I can't wait to see you tonight.

I responded with a simple smiley face emoji and

put down my phone, my face suddenly matching the expression of the picture that I sent to him. *Okay*, I thought. Maybe I could give him some leeway about this whole portfolio thing, especially when he sent messages like that.

"Wow, your place is gorgeous," I said, stepping into Craig's Brixton flat for the first time and marveling at his open-floor-plan two-bedroom apartment that featured a balcony spanning the width of his living room to his kitchen. The extra-wide, glass sliding doors to get to the balcony greeted you as soon as you walked in, providing tons of light, and, in our case at one o'clock on a Saturday morning, moonlight that flooded the walls of the flat. It was incredibly captivating and seemed to somehow match everything I knew about Craig already—modern, simple, carefree and still very connected to the fabric of the neighborhood he called home.

"Not as gorgeous as you," he responded, tracing small nibbles on the back of my neck as we slipped off our shoes at the door.

True to his word, Craig had found a way to have his mouth on some part of my body the whole night, whether it was his lips on mine as we danced, the kisses he placed on my hand while we waited at the bar for drinks or the opportunity he took to glide his tongue over the top of my chest—just above the meaty part of my cleavage—while we attempted to decide if we'd walk back to his place or catch a cab. That decision obviously took a lot longer than it needed to, since both our brains were struggling to move past our desire to have each other right then and there.

Somehow, we'd managed to make it back to his place. But I still wasn't entirely sure how, as my brain was caught in a fog of heat and passion and probably one too many rum punches.

"Aren't you tired of the way my skin feels on your lips at this point?" I asked while also subtly leaning my body into his to give him better access to me.

"I could never be tired of that," he whispered into my ear. "It's like my mouth craves you constantly."

With one more teasing bite on the back of my earlobe, Craig flipped me around to him so that we were now standing chest to chest. Then he slid his hands to my lower back and began circling our hips together as if we were still being guided by the likes of Tems, Wizkid and Davido, as we'd been for the past several hours in one of Brixton's most famous restaurants, Rum Kitchen. Known for its Caribbean food and drinks, it was also a popular spot for dancing on a Friday night—and apparently a great place to find yourself lost in a haze of music and sexual energy.

Craig tilted his head toward mine and stared at me like a man ready to completely ravish me. And I was all too ready to oblige. I leaned my chest farther into his and dragged my tongue ever so lightly over his mouth before gripping his lower lip with my teeth and pulling him into me.

"Tell me what you want," he whispered as our breathing grew heavier and more intense, both of us barely holding back from tearing the other's clothes off.

"You."

With that one-word response, Craig finally gave in to the desires he'd been struggling to hold at bay all evening. In an instant, he grabbed the back of my hair with one hand and firmly pressed his lips even deeper into mine. With our tongues still entangled, he walked us toward his balcony doors and started undressing me by first tossing my blazer off to the side. Then it was my tank top. Next, his shirt and jeans, which came off faster than I'd ever thought possible. And finally we unbuttoned my jeans together, with Craig helping to slide them down my hips, grabbing my thong underwear along with them and kissing down my stomach and thighs as he did so. By the time we reached the other side of the room, my back facing the glass doors, it was just brown skin on brown skin, with nothing left between us but my navy blue lace bra.

That didn't last long, either.

Not long after Craig stood back up, he drew me back into him and flicked open the clasp of my bra with one hand. While his lips placed light kisses on my collarbone, he fingered my bra straps, grabbing them swiftly only to let them trickle down my arms until finally I was face-to-face with him, completely naked and exposed. And the pile of clothes he'd mentioned before was to our right, laughing at me for how fast I'd allowed it to happen—practically within minutes of coming into his home.

Craig took one more step into my space, locking eyes with me in a way that I couldn't release if I'd even wanted to. Then he scooped me up, wrapped my legs around his waist and pinned my back to the glass doors before finally, achingly sliding my body right onto his penis and diving in.

Chapter Fifteen

The faint sounds from Craig's deep breaths in my ear were the first thing I noticed when I awoke six hours later in his bed, partly due to my body's investment-firm alarm clock that wouldn't let me sleep past 7:00 a.m. As I got my bearings, I first recognized the warmth from his arms and bedcovers wrapped tightly around me. Then it was the delicious remnants of his musky cologne, a scent that I seemed to have perfect access to, since my face was lying in the nook of his neck. The last thing that caught my attention, although it probably should have been the first, was the sun shining brightly from the uncovered balcony doors into his bedroom. That made for an instant reminder of the kind of debauchery those doors saw the night before, as my mind immediately flashed back to memories of Craig exploring every part of me.

If I'd been home, I would have likely gone back to sleep, either choosing to put on my night eye masks or dive farther under my covers. But in Craig's bed, in the middle of my sensory overload, I had two other thoughts in mind. First, what better opportunity was I going to get to gaze at him than when he was sleeping—thereby avoiding any awkward questions about why I was looking at him for so long. Sometimes, a girl just wanted to take her time to admire the man in front of her, right? Second, it had been three days since I talked to my crew, and even though they were set to arrive in London in less than a week, I could use some girlfriend time.

The tricky part to both plans, however, was that Craig's grip on me was like a kid with his favorite blanket. So, carefully and slowly, making sure not to wake him up, I began unfolding myself from his grasp by sliding myself just slightly to the right of him, inch by inch, until I was able to move without risk. Then I turned my body just a smidge, grabbed my phone from his nightstand and repositioned myself so that my head was lying comfortably on his pillow, with full view of my entertainment. Once I'd settled back in, I unlocked my phone and headed straight to the WhatsApp message chain that had been my lifeline since I moved.

Ladies, I typed furiously. I want you to know that you are currently receiving this message from a woman who is completely sprung, lying in bed, watching this glorious man from Brixton sleep like a baby in front of her.

Seconds later, I got the first response, from Reagan.

Reagan: The only reason I'm responding to this text at 2:00 a.m. is because that's wild AF.

I know, I replied, giggling softly to myself and dragging my eyes over Craig's chest as it rose and fell in a rhythm. It's shocking to me, too.

Jennifer: Does this mean we get to meet the famous Mr. Craig when we touch down next week?

That's very possible. I really, really like this one, I replied.

Reagan: Yeah, cher, we can really, really tell.

Jennifer: Does he know that you may not have biological siblings, but you have three sisters who will cut him if he hurts you?

Yes lol. He also seems to have his own sister who will do the same.

Reagan: That helps, but Olivia still needs to be vetted, too. I love how great a friend she's been, but I need to put my eyes on her in person, you know what I mean?

Jennifer: We need to make sure her energy is right, for sure.

   You're all going to love her. It's like having a slice of you here, I typed and then immediately felt the need to clarify. But of course, not like as a replacement for you guys. You know what I mean.

Jennifer: We understand. It's okay.

Reagan: Sure, of course. As long as everyone across the pond knows that in a week, your actual besties will be there—I'm totally fine with you having other friends in the meantime lol

Ha-ha, funny. Okay, but honestly, I can't wait to see y'all. I miss you terribly.

Jennifer: We miss you, too, Rob.

Reagan: More than we could ever say.

Rebecca: The real question is are you still staring at that man like a psycho while you're texting us?

Reagan: Oh, look who decided to join us finally!

Rebecca: Sorry, Ollie and I just got home from the club. We were getting ready for bed when we heard my phone vibrating, and he says, you already know who it is, go talk to your friends and then make sure when you come back to bed, you don't have any of those clothes on.

Reagan: Go Oliver!

Robin: Becs, how is it that your sex life is still hotter than everyone else's even while you and Oliver are trying to make a baby?

Reagan: Speak for yourself. Tuh.

Jennifer: Ditto actually. Nick and I have been taking a lot of pointers from the class of Becs Incorporated lately.

OMG, I typed, rolling my eyes. Well, never mind. I guess it's only hotter than mine then.

Rebecca: Well, isn't one of the ways to make a baby by having sex? So, why would we stop having fun because now there's a goal involved? But also, didn't you just tell us you were wrapped in the arms of a beautiful man while texting us? I wouldn't call that dull.

I'm not in his arms right now, but fair. And actually, the things we did last night in front of his balcony have to be illegal in at least 10 states back home.

Jennifer: Okay, yeah, no thanks. Don't need that imagery.

This coming from someone taking Becs Incorporated classes?! The nerve.

Jennifer: Yeah, but you're my best friend. It's not the same.

Okay, well, whatever. My only point was going to be that I AM NOT at Becs's level yet, but with Craig, that might very well change. There is just something about him that makes me want to surrender my entire body to him at all times. So, I don't know, maybe I'm starting to get those feels Becs talks about all the time.

Jennifer: Okay, now I really need to meet this man. Anyone who's got our dear Rob gushing like this has to be thoroughly examined by the crew.

I'll do my best, I typed.

Reagan: I don't think that was a request.

Rebecca: It wasn't. Plus, it'll be your birthday week. If he doesn't show up for at least one thing, I'm not going to be a happy camper.

You're right. You're all right. I'll tell him to come through. It is a little scary having you all meet him before he's official, though.

Jennifer: Official shmicial, that man's got you sprung,

boo. So, call him whatever you want, just make sure he's in our presence in a week.

Reagan: And now that Jenny has laid down the law, some of us have to go to bed. We love you, cher. See you in T-minus 6 days.

Jennifer: Yes, love you to the moon & back.

Rebeca: I love you, too. But stop staring at that man before he calls the cops on you.

Love y'all, and maybe, I replied with a huge grin on my face, thinking about all the shenanigans we were going to get into in less than a week.

For now, though, I guessed I'd given myself enough gazing time, as I was ready to snuggle back into Craig's embrace. With another quick twist of my body, I slipped my phone onto his nightstand and repositioned myself again, curling into his chest so that I could fall back asleep in his arms.

"Did you tell the girls I said hi," he asked in a whisper, wrapping his arms tightly around me almost as soon as my skin touched his.

"How long have you been awake?"

"Mmm. *Awake* is a strong word, but I felt a difference as soon as you wiggled out from under me."

"Wow, so basically the whole time then."

"Yeah, guess so. But then I also heard you on your phone and didn't want to interrupt."

"Why? Because you assumed I was gushing about you?"

"You're telling me you weren't?"

Even without looking into his face, I could hear the smirk on it. It was both annoying and addictive—just like the night we first met.

"Maybe."

"You were. But I do the same with my friends. They're all trying to figure out what spell you put on me."

"Okay, that's really funny."

Since I knew he was awake, or at least partly, I took the opportunity to shift my body even closer into him so that by the time I stopped moving, practically no parts of the fronts our bodies weren't touching. And just like that, I was back in the sweet stillness of my now-favorite sensory overload. It was the perfect morning, the two of us lying in silent contentment, letting our breaths sync together even as nothing but our chests moved—with his rising and mine falling and vice versa—building a new rhythm between us.

"What time was it when you were on your phone?" Craig asked, just as I was moments away from drifting back asleep.

"About 7:00 a.m. Why? Were you thinking about getting up and surprising me with an omelet?"

He laughed, inadvertently shaking my body as the chuckle brimmed up from his stomach.

"I would, but no. Sadly, I have to get up in a little. Have a shoot out of town."

"Oh. Like today?"

"Yeah. My flight leaves in a few hours, actually."

"How long are you going to be gone?"

"About a week."

A week?! I had no response, but suddenly, all the beautiful visions that were swirling in my head as I was drifting off to sleep just moments before turned into a deep-seated desire to kick him in his shin. How could he have forgotten to tell me he was leaving town, especially for that long? I wondered. And then to so casually say it, as if I had no right to be shocked? Maybe, I realized, that meant something even worse than him forgetting. Maybe it meant that he considered his trip need-to-know information—and I very clearly wasn't on the exclusive list of people who needed to know. Just like he didn't think it was important to tell me that he was working with my team.

"If it's any consolation, I wish I wasn't leaving."

It wasn't, I thought to myself.

"I'd rather stay here holding you all day."

Normally, with Craig, words like that would have melted my hardened heart. This time, however, I was too busy flashing back to him telling me how he was used to using the women in his life as some kind of comfort blanket whenever he happened to be home from a shoot. At the time, I'd taken it as a sign of him opening up to me about regrets from his past. Now? As I lay in his arms—with him holding me tightly—the familiar patterns felt too similar to brush off. Whatever he'd thought he'd evolved from was still very much there—maybe lingering on the surface, maybe deeply rooted, but definitely not in the past.

I didn't know what to do as I contemplated all the ways that I'd likely, once again, made a fool of myself, this time being the worst, since I knew better. If I was being generous, I'd say that we just weren't on the same page. And that, somehow, despite my intentions, I'd been the one to fall for him while he was still viewing us at a very early stage of dating. After all, as I'd said to my friends, we were not official yet, so maybe he just felt like some things were girlfriend privileges, and I wasn't his girlfriend. The ungenerous thought had him as a typical player who'd learned how to make women feel especially comfortable with him, convince them that he saw them as an exception, all to make it easier to get what he wanted. I didn't want to believe the last thought, but I couldn't stop it from nagging me.

The truth, though, was that no matter which Craig I was lying next to, the day we met, all signs pointed to *run*, and I should have listened. Instead, I'd started to trust him, fall for him, even begun to, ever so hesitantly, think about what a future could look like. That was no one's fault but my own, but one fact I knew was that I wasn't going back to being that sad girl in my mirror again. Which meant I needed to do one very important thing, quite immediately: protect myself at all costs.

I wouldn't leave. I wasn't going to cut out and run, because maybe, just maybe… I was wrong. But I also couldn't willingly keep running toward the fire. I had to slow things down on my end or I'd be the one getting burned.

"You all right?" Craig asked me, presumably either noticing my lack of a response to him or the way my body pulled away ever so slightly.

"Yeah, just thinking."

"Can I ask about what? You got real quiet on me all of a sudden."

"Maybe later," I said, moving my head to his pillow again. "Don't you have to get up and get ready?"

Craig sighed and tried to search my face, but I was no longer in his trance, so my eyes stayed right where they were—pointing to the bed.

"Yeah, I guess I should get up and take a shower."

He groaned as he released his arms from around me and began climbing out of bed. With one last heave, he lifted himself up and started walking to his bathroom.

"No chance I can convince you to join me, huh?" Craig asked, turning back around right before he reached the bathroom door to try to connect with me once again. His eyes were tired and maybe a little sad, but he still flashed his signature crooked smile in an attempt to lay on the charm. "Give me something to think about while I'm gone?"

"I'm pretty tired, actually," I replied, drawing the covers up over me so that I was almost completely hidden from his view. "I think I'm going to take a quick nap while you do that, and then I'll make sure to be ready to leave before you do."

"You can stay as long as you like. It's not like you'd be bothering anyone."

"I appreciate that, but I need to go back home. I can only stay in your cocoon so long."

"Okay," he relented. "But don't leave before I get out of the shower."

"I won't," I said, finally meeting his waiting eyes. "Trust me."

Those words lingered in my head as Craig turned back around and walked into his bathroom. Two little words that could mean so much and so little, depending on who said them. The question of the morning was now, what side was Craig on? And how would I maneuver myself differently until I found out?

Chapter Sixteen

The following Friday evening, Olivia and I left work around 6:00 p.m. and made our way over to Dirty Martini like we'd done so many times before. On this occasion, however, she was finally going to be meeting my best friends in the whole entire world.

Once inside, we passed through the frenzied crowd gathered around the main bar until, like a cave opening up to light, we saw the row of large booth tables and the three very American women sitting at the first one. In their hands were the finest of martini drinks, as they sipped and laughed and were presumably waiting for me to arrive.

"Oh my God, you're finally here!" Reagan screamed out, almost dropping her glass as she hurriedly put it down onto the table and ran toward me.

She wasn't alone in her excitement, though. As soon as I saw them, I wanted to run up to them like a kid seeing their mom after a long day at daycare, hold them tight and never let go. Reagan beat me to the punch, however. Before I could even plant my feet, she was right in my space bubble, wrapping her arms around me.

God, I'd missed them. Even just how they smelled. That wasn't something you could get through video.

"What took you so long?" she asked, her hug quickly turning from a warm embrace to a slap on my arm.

"Ouch, Rae!" I rubbed my arm to soothe it.

"Sorry, but you deserve it. We've been here since 3:00 p.m."

"Mmm-hmm," Jennifer and Rebecca moaned in agreement from where they were now standing at the table.

"I had this little thing called work to finish. I'm going to be off for the next week, so, you know, it's always a mess the day before you go on vacation."

"Mmm, okay, I guess," she said with a playful eye roll before finalizing noticing Olivia standing beside me.

"Oh my God, forgive me," she added, raising her hand to shake Liv's. "I'm Reagan. I assume you're Olivia?"

"Yes, I am," Liv said with a chuckle. "And no need to apologize. I was trying to get her to leave two hours ago."

"Et tu, Liv?"

She shrugged her shoulders in response, only

mouthing *You know it's true* in her attempt to defend the betrayal that had only taken her two minutes to come up with.

"Don't mind her, Olivia," Reagan replied as the three of us walked back to the table. "She just doesn't like being wrong."

"Don't I know it?"

"Okay, but who likes being wrong?"

"Certainly not my bestie," Jennifer chimed in as she reached in and gave me a superlong, superwarm and supercomforting hug. "But that's why we love you, boo."

"That, and your amazing cocktail-making skills," Rebecca added as she finally took her turn to squeeze me tightly.

"Did you guys come all the way to London to make fun of me for eight and a half days?"

"Of course not—we're here to celebrate our boo's thirty-first birthdaaaaay," Jennifer said with a squeal.

"And to also make fun of you," Reagan added with a laugh.

"And…to be fair, because you took so long to meet up with us, it's now more like eight days," said Rebecca.

"Okay, I'm leaving," I joked. "Hope you all know where you can get good hotels!"

"Oh, sit down, Ms. Dramatics," said Reagan, gesturing to the booth. "You know we love, love, love you, and we will gladly take any sliver of time you have for us.

"Don't judge us, Olivia," she added, turning her attention back to the lone British guest of honor. "It's just so much fun messing with her."

"No judgment at all. I'm over here taking pointers in my head."

"It's not even ten minutes in, and you're already corrupting my new friends," I chimed in as the five of us finally sat down—Olivia and Jennifer choosing to sit on the stools, and the rest of us settling into the booth. I sat on the corner side of the booth to be next to both Liv and the others.

"You say corrupting, we say getting to know each other..." Reagan replied.

"Potato, potahto," added Jennifer.

"Tomato, tomahto," finished Rebecca.

"It's all the same, yes, yes, I know," I said, joining in with another roll of my eyes. "Fine!"

I picked up the menu as if I didn't already know what I wanted while Olivia sat on her stool, still laughing at our ridiculousness. Most friends would have spent the first fifteen minutes hugging and crying and saying how much they missed each other. Especially considering—barring times of travel—three out of the four of us had never missed a week over the past thirteen years. But not mine; my crew was all about laughter and jokes, until or if things needed to get serious. Then we were obviously immediately there for each other, ready to ride out and protect anyone, just as long as we could eventually find a moment to return to laughter. It's how we handled everything from Reagan quitting her job suddenly to Christine's death to my breakup with Eric.

Essentially, in our group, we let you cry, release, get it all out—but you weren't going to stay stuck in it. Not if any of us had anything to do with it. And as much as I was fake protesting their way of loving on me, it was exactly what I needed.

I passed the menu to Olivia for her to also pretend like she didn't already know what she wanted.

"I'm having the spiced apple martini, Rae is having the wild strawberry martini and Becs is having the lavender and elderflower pink lemonade," Jenn replied, answering for everyone as Liv passed me back the menu.

"You already know I'm getting the L'amour," she whispered toward me.

"Ha-ha, true," I laughed and then scrunched my face as it hit me exactly what Jenn had said. "Wait, repeat what Becs is having again."

"A lavender and elderflower pink lemonade," she said slowly.

"As in the mocktail?"

"The very one."

"Rebecca Cunningham," I said, shifting my body to make sure I was directly facing her on the other side of the booth. "Does this mean what I think it means?"

"Well, it's very early…but yes!"

"Oh my God, Becs!"

"I know, it's wild, right?" added Reagan.

"I'm so, so happy for you, friend. This is incredible," I squealed, jumping up and down in my seat. I knew Rebecca and her husband had been trying for months, so this was definitely a moment worthy of celebration. My happiness for her was even enough to push down the brief thoughts I had about obviously being the last to know. This was one of the cons of choosing to move thousands of miles away from your best friends, I chided myself, and then quickly remembered the moment was about her and not me.

"I'm going to be an auntie for the first time ever!" I added.

Okay, maybe it could be a little bit about me.

"I can't believe Oliver let you leave his sight with this kind of news!"

"I threatened to divorce him if he tried to stop me," she joked.

"Aw, naw, it's too late to divorce now. You've trapped this man with a kid," Reagan chimed in to rounds of laughter from the table.

"Well…this might change some of the things I wanted us to do while you are all here, but it's worth it," I said as we all calmed back down.

In the same moment, the waiter stopped by and took my and Olivia's orders and second-round requests from Rae and Jenn. When he left our table again, Reagan was the first to speak up.

"Do you have a whole itinerary for us, *cher*?" she asked.

"Not exactly. Just a list of things I want us to do… and the days when it might make the most sense to do them."

"Chile, so yes, then," Jenn laughed. "Never change, friend."

"Whatever, hear me out."

"Please, go ahead."

"Thank you," I said, flashing a smile before continuing. "So, I definitely want to take you guys to Mama's Jerk. It's this Caribbean spot where the jerk chicken wraps and fries are to die for. Then, I was thinking we have to go to Ballie Ballerson, which is this super-fun, glow-in-the-dark ball pit pool bar in Shoreditch. That one we might have to amend, Becs, sorry. Next on my list was going to a Bollywood cabaret club, then afternoon tea at one of my favorite spots, karaoke, of course, a couple rooftop bars—including one at night in a car park, a dinner cruise on the Thames River—"

"Wow, this list is extensive," Jenn interjected. "When do we sleep?"

"I wasn't done, actually."

"Oh, I figured," she said with a laugh. "But for us, you were."

"Better question—when do we get to meet Craig in this very thorough list of yours?" Rebecca asked.

"Um…"

I started speaking and then looked toward Liv, who had inconveniently muttered "uh-oh" under her breath right as I was trying to get my words together.

"What do you mean, 'uh-oh'?" Reagan asked, everyone's attention now turning immediately to Olivia.

Faced with being in the spotlight because of her slip of the tongue, Liv looked back at me, her lips turning up into a cringey expression that was equal parts *sorry* and *what do I say now?*

"Things have kind of cooled down," I admitted, deciding to face my own music with my friends despite it being brought on by Liv's whisper that somehow traveled across the table.

"But six days ago, you were texting us from his bed, gushing to us about him while you gazed at what I imagined to be his very naked body," said Rebecca before turning to Liv to apologize. "Sorry, I know it's your brother and all."

"No, it's fine. I've been in the room with them and wanted to find a fire hose to cool them down. Nothing you could say would be worse than that."

"I was, yes," I responded, purposefully ignoring Olivia's side note.

"So, what happened?" Reagan asked.

"And why are we just hearing about it now?" Jennifer added.

"Six days!" Rebecca shouted in return.

"I mean, if you want the real deal, I was kind of embarrassed."

"To be honest with us?" Jennifer asked with a small tear in her eye. "You never have to worry about—"

"To admit that I moved too fast in my own head. But anyway, it's not over, *exactly*, I'm just backing things up on my end."

"What does that mean?" asked Rebecca.

I sighed, thinking that this was just why I hadn't wanted to bring up the subject of Craig. We were a loving crew, yes, but also annoyingly persistent at times. Liv must have read my body language, because unlike before, she quickly jumped in to respond.

"From what I can tell, it just means that she's not really initiating things with him anymore or making herself available all the time when he calls or texts. Did I get that right?" she asked, looking my way with sympathetic eyes.

"Something like that. I mean, for example, he's out of town right now—or he might have come back today, I can't remember—but there have been a few times when he wanted to stay up and talk all night like…before…and I just told him that I couldn't."

"So, you've completely disinvested yourself and shut down," Jennifer said matter-of-factly, clearly proving she was still seeing the therapist I'd recommended to her last year.

"Okay, therapy words," I said with a smile.

"I'm serious, Rob."

"I know you are, but honestly, guys, I don't want to do this right now. Things are what they are, and I just want to enjoy the eight and a half days I have with you."

"Eight," said Reagan with a laugh that almost turned into a snort.

I glared back at her and jokingly rolled my eyes again.

"Fine, eight. But that's all the more reason for us not to waste our precious time on something that's out of my hands."

"Okay," Jennifer said, throwing her hands up in defeat.

"But we're going to revisit this before the trip is over," added Reagan.

"Oh joy, just what I want to look forward to for my birthday."

"Speaking of birthday," Rebecca said, leaning

across the table. "Can we go back to this list again? Because I'm down for all that—even the ball pit, which I'll just make sure I read up on before we go—but honestly, I was also hoping we could have at least one day where we just chill at your place in our pj's, have Nacho Night and fully catch up with each other."

"I'm down for that," I replied, excitedly watching the waiter arrive with our drinks in hand. "What do you say we make your last day a pj's-in-the-flat day and Nacho Night evening?"

"The last day meaning your birthday?" Jenn asked for clarification.

"Yes, one and the same."

"So, you'd be fine with a simple birthday celebration, then? Just us hanging out?"

"Absolutely."

"Because just last year, you planned an epic extravaganza for our thirtieth…" Jennifer added, continuing her interrogation.

"Oh, did I plan that alone?"

"Okay, maybe not," she laughed. "But you were definitely the leader of it all."

"Sure, but that was thirty. You only get to celebrate that once. And if we make it through everything I want to do on this list, we'll probably be tired by my birthday anyway."

"Okay! If you're down, then I'm down," she exclaimed.

"Let's do it!" added Rebecca.

"Yes! Nacho Thursdays!" Reagan shrieked as she also reached for her drink and placed it on the table.

"Wait, isn't your birthday next Friday, Rob?" Olivia asked with a confused look on her face.

"Oh, Olivia, we have so much to teach you," Jennifer replied with a smile. She then made a face toward me that quickly but very seriously said, *We'll address her using your nickname later*, before turning back to Liv with her previous joyous expression.

"The first of which is that Nacho Thursdays are rarely if ever on Thursdays," she continued. "We started doing them as a way to make sure we had definitive plans to see each other at least once a week, and I think maybe they started off on Thursdays, hence the name. But with our jobs and different obligations, we eventually needed to be more flexible—so the name stuck, but the day can actually be any day of the week."

"And really, it's kind of more fun when it's not on a Thursday. It becomes our little inside joke," Reagan added with an eyebrow raised in my direction.

"*Ohhh*, okay. I get it now," Liv replied, seemingly none the wiser at the nonverbal signals my friends were sending my way about her use of "Rob."

"So, to Nacho Thursdays…" Rebecca said, lifting her mocktail in the air.

"On a Friday!" Liv quickly replied with a look that showed how much fun she realized it was to finish sentences in our group. She raised her glass in the air, too, before saying one more thing. "While you're here, I have something to teach you lot, too."

We all sat silently with very serious expressions plastered on our faces, worried and waiting to see what she would say next. She'd already inadvertently spilled the beans on two things in less than an hour—what more could she have to say? I thought.

"In the UK, we don't toast without saying one very important word."

"And that is?" Rebecca asked with relief.

"Cheers!"

Olivia's smile lit up her face as everyone else relaxed theirs. We all immediately picked our glasses up to meet hers in the air.

"Say less, Olivia," Jennifer replied.

"Please, call me Liv."

"Say less, Liv."

"Cheers!" everyone shouted in unison as our glasses clinked together.

Then, after making sure to take at least one sip of our drinks, we also looked everyone in the eyes, so as not to risk seven years of bad sex. No one at the table was exactly superstitious, but why take the chance? As Jennifer put her glass down, she eyed mine with a quizzical expression.

"Wait, Rob, what did you order? It's not what I think it is, is it?" she asked.

"It's a black cherry and pomegranate spritz with a prosecco floater," I said with a smile.

"You mean to tell me that the sibling to your extremely intricate Robin special is actually on the menu?"

"Kinda," I laughed. "They have the black cherry and pomegranate spritz on the menu, and I always ask them to add the floater."

"*Of couuurse* you do," shouted Reagan.

I shrugged my shoulders.

"Joke all you want, but it works!"

"Honestly, I'm impressed. You…our dear Rob… found something that wasn't *exactly* perfect and worked with it, and now you love it so much that you get it all the time. Huh? Interesting."

"Ugh," I said with yet another roll eye. "Waiter, can I get another drink, please! These girls over here are trying to drive me insane."

"We love you!" Jennifer pleaded.

"Uh-huh," I replied. "I'm still going to need that drink, though."

"Wake up, sunshine, it's your birthday!"

Rolling over in bed, I slowly took off my night mask and attempted to open one eye and then the next. As my vision started coming to, I looked in the direction of the giggling voices and vaguely saw three figures in pajamas and tiaras peeking into my bedroom door.

"What time is it?" I asked.

"Around 10:00 a.m."

"What?!"

I shot up in my bed, shocked I'd slept in so late.

"I know. We were almost concerned, but we unanimously decided you just needed your rest, so we didn't want to wake you," Jennifer replied.

"Until now," added Reagan.

I looked into the now very clear, very obviously plotting eyes of my best friends and wondered what was next.

"Why now?" I asked hesitantly.

"Well, we finished cooking and we didn't want it to get cold," Rebecca responded, as they finally all fully walked into my room with what they were hiding behind them now visible: a breakfast platter holding a huge omelet, bacon, muffins and a glass of orange juice.

I am blessed with some truly amazing friends, I thought to myself.

"Happy birthdaaaaaay!" they shouted, jumping onto my bed as Rebecca placed the platter on my nightstand.

"You guys..."

"Do not even begin to protest," Reagan said, interrupting me as she slid a tiara onto my head.

"It's your birthday, my love!" added Jennifer.

"And so, we may be keeping it chill today, but no one said we had to be ragamuffins about it," Reagan chimed in.

"Ragamuffins?!" Rebecca asked, turning to look at her in shock.

"Okay, whatever, y'all know I'm from the South. Just go with it."

We all shook our heads in laughter as my heart filled with joy. Reagan's Southern phrases combined with her sometimes French sayings, like calling everyone *cher*, never ceased to amaze us, and we loved her for it. Even if she was sometimes as ridiculous as she accused her mom of being.

With all our tiaras now perfectly placed on our heads, the girls began singing Stevie Wonder's rendition of "Happy Birthday," which somehow then led into the Chuck E. Cheese version, only to finally blend into Fly Boi Keno's very catchy New Orleans bounce version. I thought my face was going to explode, I was so happy. The only thing that would have made the morning more perfect was if our quartet had its fifth member still with us—because no way she'd let the moment pass by without jumping in to give her signature operatic rendition.

"I know what you're thinking," Jenn said softly, looking at me as they all settled into seated positions around me.

"What's that?" I asked suspiciously.

"We're missing one more version of the song."

"Yeah," I said, tearing up, even with my smile still genuinely plastered on my face. "We really, really are."

"We thought the same thing, but then Reagan told us she had this…"

As the room fell silent, Reagan pulled out her cell phone and played a voice mail of Christine singing "Happy Birthday" for one full minute. Her tone was impeccable, like always, but it was her voice, that voice I'd missed hearing for almost a whole year, that took me clean out. Forget tearing up, I was practically wiping globs of tears off my face as the voice mail ended. Unsurprisingly, I wasn't alone.

"Where did you…" I started to ask but then couldn't even get out all the words.

"She left it for me a couple years ago, and I guess I never erased it."

"Thank God you didn't," I said, inhaling deeply as I composed myself. "That was the perfect way to end this morning fete. Thank you, honestly."

"It was really beautiful," said Jenn. "But we're not done yet."

"You're not?"

"Absolutely not."

"First off, you have to eat this omelet that we made. I don't want toot my own horn, but I think it might just be better than Darius Lovehall's," Reagan said with a wink. "Plus, who says you have to wait for some man to make it for you to marry him, when your real soul mates are right in front of you?"

"Touché," I laughed. "Can I ask what's in it before I take a bite?"

"Yes, you may. It's a three-egg omelet with shrimp, crabmeat, peppers, onions, tomatoes, spinach and Gruyère cheese."

"Mmm, okay, that sounds delish."

They all watched me intently as I picked up the plate from my nightstand, cut the first slice of omelet and placed a piece in my mouth.

"Damn, this is really good," I mumbled with a mouthful of food.

In truth, I almost thought I was going to have a food orgasm right in front of them. Maybe Reagan was on to something after all. Why wait for a Darius when I had three Josies already surrounding me? But they were missing one key ingredient...

"The only problem is none of you has on just a pair of jeans!" I said, laughing, after I'd finished swallowing yet another bite.

"Oh, if that's all you need, I can make that happen right now," Rebecca replied.

"No, no," I said stopping her just as she was getting ready to crawl out of the bed. "I was only joking. I don't need anything else, honestly. I have all that I need right here."

And I wasn't lying. As I looked at the three women sitting cross-legged on my bed, I realized how loved I was already by some of the best people I ever met, and on the morning of the day I turned thirty-one, they were all here for me. Maybe it wasn't the goal I'd aimed to achieve by my birthday, but it was pretty damn good.

"Wait, we did forget one thing, though!" Jenn said, jumping out of the bed and running back to my kitchen. "The champagne! That orange juice is just for show— you're not starting thirty-one drinking anything without bubbles. Don't worry, we also have sparkling cider for Preggo."

I watched with joy as she quickly returned with glasses and two bottles in her hand, purposely ignoring the vibrating phone next to my thigh showing a missed call from Craig.

True to their word, we spent the next six hours of my birthday drinking champagne and sparkling cider, luxuriating around my flat in our pajamas and tiaras, and dancing to a playlist of all Mariah Carey's remixes that included iconic hits like "Breakdown" featuring Bone Thugs-N-Harmony and "Heartbreaker" featuring Da Brat and Missy Elliott, but also cult classics like "Bye Bye" with Jay-Z. It was the perfect low-key birthday celebration—only occasionally interrupted by welcome calls from my parents, coworkers, other friends and, of course, Liv.

By 4:00 p.m. however, the hunger bug started spreading among us, and we knew it was time to drag ourselves into the kitchen to start making the featured meal for the night.

"You guys didn't use all the shrimp for breakfast, right?" I asked as I started pulling out ingredients for the nachos.

"Oh no, there's more than enough still in there," Reagan answered. "That's why we supplemented with some of the lump crabmeat you already had in your fridge."

"Ah, okay, very smart!"

One by one, I plopped items from the refrigerator and then my cabinets onto the kitchen counter as Jennifer checked them off our list. By the time we were done, a big pile of tomatoes, onions, shredded cheese, salsa, shrimp, ground beef, black beans, cilantro and tortilla chips were spread across my kitchen counter. The only thing left was for us to begin prepping and cooking it all.

"I'll cook the shrimp and beef," Reagan said, pulling her items from the pile and dragging them to my stove, where two huge skillets were waiting for her.

"And I'll chop the tomatoes, onions and cilantro," added Rebecca.

"I'll get started adding the nachos and beans to the baking pans, so they're ready for the other ingredients when you two are done," said Jennifer. "Oh! And I'll keep the drinks pouring."

Looking around the kitchen, I suddenly realized there wasn't anything left for me to contribute other than preheating the oven.

"I don't think there's anything left to do," I said, scrunching my face.

"Well, that's good, considering it *is* your birthday," Rebecca replied.

"Right. Like we'd even let you do anything," added Jennifer. "I mean, except for getting the oven set up. That's all you. We're not trying to burn down your flat."

"Ha-ha. It's not that different—you just have to know the temperature conversions—but yes, of course."

I scooched my way around Rebecca as she began chopping the tomatoes and turned the oven on so that it would be ready for our four baking pans of nachos—two shrimp and two beef—once they were prepped. With that out of the way, I grabbed my champagne flute again and walked toward the entryway of the kitchen to keep it from feeling too cramped for the people actually doing the work.

"There is one more thing you can do," said Reagan as she seasoned the beef and shrimp in two separate bowls.

I took a sip of my drink and waited for her to continue.

"You can finally tell us what's going on with you and Craig."

"Ugh, I should have known this was a setup."

"It's not a setup," she replied. "But it is our last day,

and we said we'd discuss things before we left. No time better than the present to address the elephant in the room."

"Okay, fine," I said before taking a large gulp of my champagne and effectively finishing off my latest glass. "What do you want to know?"

"For starters, what happened? It can't just be that he went out of town."

"It's not," I said, feeling the tears start to threaten. "But the fact that he didn't think to tell me—it just woke me up from the dream world I'd been in with him. You guys know after all my failed attempts at dating and relationships, I can usually spot a red flag a mile away. And his was staring me in my face the whole time, but I was missing it. Ultimately, I just don't know if he actually wants a relationship. He may want to be with me, but that's not the same thing."

"And have you asked him about this?" Rebecca asked.

She'd almost finished chopping three tomatoes as if she was a master chef and was moving onto the last one before tackling the cilantro and then the onions.

"I mean…"

"So, that's a no," she interrupted.

"I don't know what I'd need to ask him. If I've learned anything, it's that actions speak louder than words. That doesn't necessarily mean he's a bad guy, but if I'm looking at his actions, he's told me everything I need to know. Is it so horrible that I'm taking him at that?"

"It is if you're so haunted by your history of red

flags that you're seeing them when they may not even be there," said Reagan. "I'm not saying you're wrong to be scared, but what's the harm in just asking him?"

"I already know what he'll say, though. Craig's got all the charm in the world. What I'm telling my best friends right now is that his actions don't match his words."

"One time, they didn't," said Jennifer. "How many times have you encouraged us to give people chances to make mistakes and do better? I wouldn't be engaged to Nick right now if I never allowed him to be human and get things wrong sometimes."

"And I wouldn't be moving to New York to be with Jake," added Reagan. "You literally told him to fight for me."

"It was twice, but either way, it's not the same, you guys. You're talking about men you have a history with, who'd already proven their love for you when they messed up."

"You think that made things easier?" asked Reagan. "I can tell you it absolutely did not."

"I'm not saying it was easy. I'm saying you had a foundation to build on. With Craig, as much as I like him, and as much as I really did want things to work, I just can't stop asking myself, 'What's the worst that could happen?' if I...trust him. And because we haven't known each other that long, and there's no history telling me otherwise, my brain can come up with a list the size of a CVS receipt—beginning with me being heartbroken once again, this time without you all around to support me while I try to pick myself up."

"That would never happen," said Reagan as she dumped the ground beef into the first skillet and then turned to look me in my eyes. "I don't care where you live, we will always be here for each other. No matter what."

"We made a whole vow last year that this friendship is built to last, no matter where we go or who we end up with," Jennifer added. "Did you forget that already?"

"No, I remember," I said, wiping the tears that had started flowing down my face. "But a vow doesn't make that ocean any smaller."

"So, are you telling us you regret moving here?" Rebecca asked.

"I'm not. I love it here, and as much as I miss you three, I think it's one of the best decisions I've made in a while. I just… I don't know if I'm strong enough to make it through another heartbreak without you."

"But Rob, hear me out," said Reagan, "I don't think our home addresses are what's stopping you. It's your fear. But fear doesn't have to stop you—it can push you and inspire you to move past it. I mean, what if, for once, instead of focusing on all the things that could go wrong with a guy, you asked yourself what essentially you always ask us, 'What's the *best* that could happen?'"

"That would certainly be a change," I said, sniffing my tears dry.

"Yeah, it would be," Reagan replied softly.

Just then, the beef in the skillet began sizzling loudly, reminding her that she needed to stir it. And Jennifer seemed to take the sudden silence in the room as her cue to pull another bottle out of the refrigerator now that she'd finished her baking-pan prep. With a quick twist of her wrist, she freed the next cork, somehow knowing how to have it make only a slight *tssh* sound.

Rebecca, having finished chopping everything, turned to me and smiled.

"You okay?" she asked.

"Yeah, just have a lot to think about now."

"Okay, well, can I ask you one more question?"

"Why not," I said, throwing up my hands.

"Have you heard from him at all since we've been here? I know we've said this a lot now, but it *is* your birthday. Don't get me wrong, I agree with Rae's assessment, but I'm kind of shocked he hasn't called you. Unless he has."

"Well…"

"Rob?" They all shifted their bodies and asked in unison.

"He may have called a few times," I responded quickly under my breath.

"Give me this phone," Reagan said, maneuvering her way past Jenn and Becs to get to me. She grabbed the phone out of my hand before I had a chance to stop her, opened it and went directly to my missed calls.

"Robin Johnson," she said, staring at my phone in horror. "Robin Bridget Johnson!"

"How many times has he called?" Rebecca asked.

Reagan used her fingers to scroll down my call log as she responded.

"Today alone, four times."

"Robin!" Jennifer screamed out.

"But in the past week, four more…no, five more times."

Still clutching the phone in her hand and moving on to my text messages app, Reagan glared in my direction like a momma highly disappointed in her kid. She quickly found his name and began scrolling through our text chain as well, looking for the last time I'd replied to him. It had been Wednesday.

"He's also texted her a number of times, too," she said out loud to everyone, thankfully choosing to keep the rest to herself. She swiveled her attention back to me. "And you think these are the actions of a man not interested in you?"

"I don't know," I said with a shrug. "It's easy to call someone a bunch of times, but what is he doing to build an honest relationship with me?" I asked.

"What are you?" she asked in return, handing me my phone back. "If you want an honest relationship, Rob, you've got to participate in that, too. Fears be damned."

"Mmm-hmm," moaned Jennifer. "You have to take your own advice, baby girl. No convincing can also mean it's time to stop convincing yourself every man is out to hurt you and finally give one a chance to get to know you. Because if you do, I already know he's going to love you like we all do."

"All right, if I agree to think about it, can we move on to other conversations?" I asked.

"You bet," Jennifer replied.

"Okay, good."

"Oh, I have one," Rebecca added as she began mixing her intricately chopped tomatoes, onions and cilantro in a large bowl. Once Reagan added the shrimp and beef to their respective baking pans, Becs's job was going to be to take that mixed bowl and divide it into four, gently tossing the ingredients on top. "So, Rob is, like, a universal nickname now?"

I knew this one would come up eventually. I hadn't predicted it would be from Rebecca, though, who herself had to be added to the list of approved people to use it when she started hanging out with us a couple years ago.

"I'm sorry!" I shrieked, lifting the corners of my lips into a cringe. "But you see how wonderful she is. It was hard to resist when she told me to call her Liv. I kinda felt like I needed to offer mine up, too."

"Hmm. I mean, she is wonderful," Reagan said, draining the beef and finishing her last toss of the shrimp in their skillet. "But it would have been nice to just know you were letting her call you that. That's all. It used to be only our thing."

"I know, and you're right. I should have said something."

"It's fine," Jennifer said, jokingly rolling her eyes. "We seem to have this horrible affliction of actually loving you, so it's not like we can be mad when others do, too."

I smiled brightly and jumped to give them all hugs.

"Thanks, guys. I'm glad you understand. And that you like her. I really wanted you to."

"Of course we do. She's everything you said she

would be. Plus, I kinda like having someone around who's closer to my age," Rebecca interjected, remarking on the fact that she was five years older than Reagan, Jennifer and I and Liv was four.

"Yay!"

Reagan began pouring the proteins onto the pans, with Rebecca sliding behind her and tossing the veggies on perfectly. It was nice to see that our assembly line for nacho making hadn't been lost in the months since I'd been in London. Once all four pans were prepped, they placed them in the oven, closed the door and set the timer for fifteen minutes.

"And now, we drink and wait," I said, turning to head into the living room.

The girls followed me, glasses in hand and bellies waiting in full anticipation.

Chapter Seventeen

"It feels like you just got here. I can't believe you're leaving already," I said in between a round of hugs with the girls at my front door.

"I know," Jennifer replied, dramatically turning her face into a frown. "But you'll be back in DC in June for Rae's birthday, she and I are coming for Glastonbury, and of course, we'll have a little bambina to celebrate soon enough."

"Don't forget your wedding, too!" Reagan added.

"Oh right, that, too," she laughed. "So, see? You're going to see us so much you won't even know what it feels like to miss us."

"Highly doubtful," I said. "I am going to miss you guys as soon as you walk out that door. But you're right—we'll be bothering each other and causing eye rolls again in no time."

"Speaking of eye rolls, don't forget what we said last night, please," Reagan said, grabbing her suitcase as she crossed the threshold. "You've got some thinking to do, and a couple phone calls to return."

"I hear you," I said. "Loud and clear."

The three of them piled their way out of my door, and with their roller bags at their sides, began making their way down my hallway toward the elevator. Their car to get back to the airport was already waiting for them downstairs, but we'd needed at least one more minute of goodbyes when they initially received the alert that he'd arrived. I watched them as they disappeared into the lift, the doors closing behind them. And then, with a deep inhale and exhale, I walked back into my flat, closed my front door and headed to my bedroom to find the first thing that had popped into my head when Reagan reminded me of our conversation the night before.

Once in my room, I went straight to my closet and immediately picked out the blush-pink Sophia Webster shoebox that held the angel wing stilettos Reagan had gifted me for my thirtieth birthday. Even though I'd worn them on my flight to London, I'd had the box (along with a few others) shipped to me a few weeks later so the designer heels wouldn't be exposed to the air constantly. This time, however, it wasn't the shoes that I needed from inside the box; it was the note she'd included with them. Seated on my floor, I pulled the letter out of the box and read it.

These shoes are badass, but not as badass as you.
Take the job in London. Believe in yourself a little bit. We need you, but you need this even more.

Leave it to Reagan to be right even when she wasn't
in my face. It was a simple letter, but it served as the
best reminder. I was badass. I'd said so myself when
I made the decision to come here. But I needed to be
fearless in every part of my life, including the part
that was the hardest for me—trusting someone with
my heart.

I hopped off the floor, wiped away a small tear that
had formed in my eye and knew exactly what I had to
do next. Forget calling Craig back, I thought; I needed
to see him in person, to look him in his eyes and tell
him the truth. Only then could I live up to the words
Rae had written to affirm me.

With renewed determination, I changed out of my
pajamas from the day before, hurriedly jumped in the
shower and put on a pair of jeans and a T-shirt with a
knot in the front of it in less than fifteen minutes. My
hair was already in a messy bun, so with nothing else
left to hold me up, I grabbed the note and practically
ran to my front door. I slid on the first sneakers I saw,
grabbed my keys and threw open my door—just to find
Craig standing there getting ready to knock.

"Oh! Hi," I said, shocked but delighted to see his
face.

"Hi," he said, returning my smile.

"I was just on my way to you."

"Really?"

"Yeah. I figured what I had to say I should do in person."

"Robin, look, before you end things…"

"Wait, stop. Let me talk first, okay?"

I stepped to the side so that he could walk into my apartment and closed the door behind him. In the confines of my foyer, I almost lost my nerve—until I felt the note in my hand, practically egging me on to be the fearless woman I say I am. Before I could stop myself again, I blurted out everything I could—almost in one breath.

"Craig, I'm sorry. I haven't been up front with you. I asked you to be honest with me, but ever since I learned that you were working with my team and then that you were going out of town and hadn't told me, I've been using those instances as reasons to mistrust you and to back away without doing the one thing I asked you to do. I should have said something immediately when I realized I was upset. And I should have point-blank asked you if my feelings for you were mutual, but I panicked. All I could think about was how destroyed I'd be if everything you'd said to me had been a lie, so I did what I always do—I protected myself, I put up walls and I started pushing you away so that I could justify my fears."

I inhaled deeply as he looked back at me intently, his eyes poring over me with concern. He tried to move in closer to me, but I stepped back just a bit, wanting to get everything off my chest first.

"But the thing is," I continued, "I don't want to hold on to those fears anymore. My friends reminded me yesterday how much they are keeping me from every-thing I want. So, I'm standing here now, frightened but willingly showing you my heart. Hoping that a glimpse of the real Robin hasn't scared you off."

I took one step toward him and stopped again, feeling the need to clarify one more thing. "And if it has," I said with a sigh, "that's okay, too. I know I haven't made things easy the past couple weeks, and it's not like we've known each other even that long to… Well, anyway, just know whatever your response is, it's okay."

"Are you finished now?" he asked, still eyeing me from a few feet away.

"I think so," I laughed awkwardly.

"Okay, so first of all, I didn't know that you were upset about those things. I've been literally racking my head trying to figure out what had gone wrong."

"I know, I should have—"

"No, please," he interjected. "Let me finish. I'm not upset you didn't tell me. I just wish I'd known, because then I would have told you that I didn't mention I was working with your team because I wanted to make sure you liked my work without knowing it was me. Frank had already said there was potential for me to do more but that it was up to his boss. Once I realized that was you, I didn't want you to agree to take me on as a contractor just because it was me or because I'm Liv's brother. But I didn't think of how that might come off to you, to find out from someone else, and I'm sorry for that. As far as the work trip, that's my bad. I'm new to this whole healthy-relationship thing, so I'm not always going to get that kind of stuff right, at least at first. It didn't even dawn on me that not giving you a heads-up might be a problem. You're right, though. If the tables were reversed, I probably would have been just as angry. Especially given what I've told you about my past and what I've done on work trips before you."

"I want you to be able to tell me that kind of stuff, though, and not feel like I'm going to use it against you."

"I know that. I also know it's a fair concern. But the difference between those times and now is that I don't want to be with anyone else. You've stolen my whole heart, Robin, and I'm better because of it. I can't very well take it back from you without a fight."

"Okay, what's the second of all?" I asked, curling my lips into what was becoming a joyful smirk.

"Second of all," he said, stepping fully into my space, "happy birthday. I know I'm a day late from your goal, but if you still want me, I would love it if you would do me the honor of being my girlfriend."

My smile grew to the size of Texas upon hearing the words I'd been aching to hear for so long. And somehow, they had come from the mouth of a man I had just let see the ugliest side of me—the one that pushed people away before they could hurt her—and in return, he hadn't run away. He was standing in front of me asking for more.

What's the best that could happen, indeed.

"Yes," I said with a smile. "A thousand times, yes."

Craig didn't let a second pass after my response before he scooped me up, throwing my legs around his waist. I followed my legs up with my arms, holding on to him tightly as he began walking us into my living room.

"We've got a lot to catch up on, then, girlfriend. But first, I've been missing this…"

He gently sat me on the couch and, leaning over me, placed his lips directly over mine without touching them, almost as if he was waiting for me to make the next move. I happily obliged, raising myself up just enough to press my lips into his, and then wrapped my arms around his neck as I pulled him down onto me.

"Thank God you didn't say no," he whispered in between our kisses.

"That was never an option, Craig," I replied, memories flooding my head of every interaction we'd ever had and realizing how good—no, how badass—it felt to finally let go and give my heart to him. "Not even from the very first moment we met."

* * * * *

Don't miss out on any books in
The Friendship Chronicles

The Shoe Diaries
Bloom Where You're Planted

Available now from Harlequin Special Edition!

Acknowledgments

Publishing my debut novel, The Shoe Diaries, with Harlequin Special Edition was a dream come true. Getting the opportunity to publish a second and then a third book (!!!) as part of this series is what many like to call abundant overflow. I am completely overjoyed and could not have done this without countless people by my side.

My first thanks always goes to my Creator; the one who gave me this dream in the first place and continues to show up and show out in my life. I am nothing without my relationship with God; it guides me, corrects me, and inspires me daily.

To the dream team I've been lucky enough to have around me on this book journey—my dynamic agent, Latoya C. Smith, my fabulous editor, Gail Chasan, my fantastic publicist, Dawn Michelle Hardy, and the rocks that hold it all together: Megan Broderick and Caroline Greelish, as well as everyone at Harlequin who has supported me and worked to make these books a reality—my gratitude to you all knows no end.

To my family and friends: I'm not going to set myself up by trying to list names this time lol, but I continue to be amazed at how you love me over and over again. Please know that I don't ever take it for granted. I'm forever thankful for each and every one of you, whether we met the day I was born or just recently and became fast "author friends."

And to my readers: I never realized how much joy I would get by reading and hearing that my words meant something to someone else. I only hope that I can continue to write stories that are meaningful, loving, and stir up something in your soul when you read them.

The best is yet to come! (#Nkiruka)

COMING NEXT MONTH FROM

HARLEQUIN®
SPECIAL EDITION™

#2941 THE CHRISTMAS COTTAGE
Wild Rose Sisters • by Christine Rimmer

Alexandra Herrera has her whole life mapped out. But when her birth father leaves her an unexpected inheritance, she impulsively walks away from it all. And now that she's snowed in with West Wright, she learns that lightning really *can* strike twice. So much, in fact, that the sparks between them could melt any ice storm...if only they'd let them!

#2942 THANKFUL FOR THE MAVERICK
Montana Mavericks: Brothers & Broncos • by Rochelle Alers

As a rodeo champion, Brynn Hawkins is always on the road, but something about older, gruff-but-sexy rancher Garrett Abernathy makes her think about putting down roots. As Thanksgiving approaches, Brynn fears she's running out of time, but she's determined to find her way into this calloused cowboy's heart!

#2943 SANTA'S TWIN SURPRISE
Dawson Family Ranch • by Melissa Senate

Cowboy Asher Dawson and rookie cop Katie Crosby had the worst one-night stand ever. Now she's back in town with his two babies. He won't risk losing Katie again—even as he tries to deny their explosive chemistry. But his marriage of convenience isn't going.as planned. Maybe it's time to see what happens when he moves his captivating soul mate beyond friendship...

#2944 COUNTDOWN TO CHRISTMAS
Match Made in Haven • by Brenda Harlen

Rancher Adam Morgan's hands are full caring for his ranch and three adorable sons. When his custody is challenged, remarriage becomes this divorced dad's best solution—and Olivia Gilmore doesn't mind a proposal from the man she's loved forever. But Adam is clear: this is a match made by convenience. But as jingle bells give way to wedding bells, will he trust in love again?

#2945 SECRET UNDER THE STARS
Lucky Stars • by Elizabeth Bevarly

When his only love, Marcy Hanlon, returns, Max Tavers believes his wish is coming true. But Marcy has different intentions—she secretly plans to expose Max as the cause of her wealthy family's downfall! She'll happily play along and return his affections. But if he's the reason her life went so wrong, why does being with him feel so right?

#2946 A SNOWBOUND CHRISTMAS COWBOY
Texas Cowboys & K-9s • by Sasha Summers

Rodeo star Sterling Ford broke Cassie Lafferty's heart when he chose a lifestyle of whiskey and women over her. Now the reformed party boy is back, determined to reconnect with the woman who got away. When he rescues Cassie and her dogs from a snowstorm, she learns she isn't immune to Sterling's smoldering presence. But it'll take a canine Christmas miracle to make their holiday romance permanent!

YOU CAN FIND MORE INFORMATION ON UPCOMING HARLEQUIN TITLES, FREE EXCERPTS AND MORE AT HARLEQUIN.COM.

HSECNM0922

*By the book success story Alexandra Herrera's got it
all mapped out. But when her birth father leaves her
an unexpected inheritance, she impulsively walks away
from her entire life! And now that she's snowed in with
West Wright, she learns that lightning really can strike
twice. So much, in fact, that the sparks between them
could melt any ice storm...if only they'd let them!*

Read on for a sneak peek at
The Christmas Cottage,
the latest in the Wild Rose Sisters series
by New York Times *bestselling author Christine Rimmer!*

So that was an option, just to say that she needed her alone
time and West would intrude on that. Everyone would
understand. But then he would stay at the Heartwood Inn
and that really wasn't right...

And what about just telling everyone that it would be
awkward because she and West had shared a one-night
stand? There was nothing unacceptable about what she
and West had done. No one here would judge her. Alex
and West were both adults, both single. It was nobody's
business that they'd had sex on a cold winter night when
he'd needed a friend and she was the only one around
to hold out a hand. It was one of those things that just
happen sometimes.

It would be weird, though, to share that information
with the family. Weird and awkward. And Alex still
hoped she would never have to go there.

"Alex?" Weston spoke again, his voice so smooth and deep and way too sexy.

"Hmm?"

"You ever plan on answering my question?"

"Absolutely." It came out sounding aggressive, almost angry. She made herself speak more cordially. "Yes. Honestly. There's plenty of room here. You're staying in the cottage. It's settled."

"You're so bossy…" He said that kind of slowly— slowly and also naughtily—and she sincerely hoped her cheeks weren't cherry red.

"Weston." She said his name sternly as a rebuke.

"Alexandra," he mocked.

"That's a yes, right?" Now she made her voice pleasant, even a little too sweet. "You'll take the second bedroom."

"Yes, I will. And it's good to talk to you, Alex. At last." Did he really have to be so…ironic? It wasn't like she hadn't thought more than once of reaching out to him, checking in with him to see how he was holding up. But back in January, when they'd said goodbye, he'd seemed totally on board with cutting it clean. "Alex? You still there?"

"Uh, yes. Great."

"See you day after tomorrow. I'll be flying down with Easton."

"Perfect. See you then." She heard the click as he disconnected the call.

Don't miss
The Christmas Cottage *by Christine Rimmer,*
available November 2022 wherever
Harlequin Special Edition books and ebooks are sold.

Harlequin.com

HARLEQUIN

Heartfelt or thrilling, passionate or uplifting—Harlequin is more than just happily-ever-after.

With twelve different series to choose from and new books available every month, you are sure to find stories that will move you, uplift you, inspire and delight you.

Love Harlequin romance?

DISCOVER.

Be the first to find out about promotions, news and exclusive content!

Facebook.com/HarlequinBooks

Twitter.com/HarlequinBooks

Instagram.com/HarlequinBooks

Pinterest.com/HarlequinBooks

YouTube.com/HarlequinBooks

ReaderService.com

EXPLORE.

Sign up for the Harlequin e-newsletter and download a free book from any series at **TryHarlequin.com**

CONNECT.

Join our Harlequin community to share your thoughts and connect with other romance readers!
Facebook.com/groups/HarlequinConnection